J. T. Conners was born in Calgary, Alberta, Canada. At a young age, she moved with her small family to the Shuswap area within British Columbia, Canada, where she grew to love the beauty of nature. J. T. now resides within Alberta, with the love of her life and her two sons, in a small town just outside of Calgary. J. T. has always had a passion for singing, theatre, and writing. In the days when there was no internet, cell phones, or gaming consoles, J. T. would fill her teenage hours with dirt-biking in the mountains with her beloved dog, Tess, and writing stories by hand. J. T. fell in love with writing romance novels when her grandmother passed away and found her basement packed full of love stories her grandmother had read over the years.

To Brian, for continuing to believe in me, even with all my crazy intricacies. To my sons, Aidan and Dalon, who challenge me daily to be the best mother that I can be. To my mom, Mildred, who has always shown strength and resilience so I could become the woman that I am today, and finally to my soul sisters, Mandy, Shana and Lisa, for always putting up with my incessant babbling and bizarre escapades. My love knows no bounds.

J. T. Conners

UNNATURAL BEGINNINGS

The Adam and Eve Project

AUSTIN MACAULEY PUBLISHERS™
LONDON • CAMBRIDGE • NEW YORK • SHARJAH

Copyright © J. T. Conners 2022

All rights reserved. No part of this publication may be reproduced, distributed, or transmitted in any form or by any means, including photocopying, recording, or other electronic or mechanical methods, without the prior written permission of the publisher, except in the case of brief quotations embodied in critical reviews and certain other non-commercial uses permitted by copyright law. For permission requests, write to the publisher.

Any person who commits any unauthorized act in relation to this publication may be liable to criminal prosecution and civil claims for damages.

This is a work of fiction. Names, characters, businesses, places, events, locales, and incidents are either the products of the author's imagination or used in a fictitious manner. Any resemblance to actual persons, living or dead, or actual events is purely coincidental.

Ordering Information
Quantity sales: Special discounts are available on quantity purchases by corporations, associations, and others. For details, contact the publisher at the address below.

Publisher's Cataloging-in-Publication data
Conners, J. T.
Unnatural Beginnings

ISBN 9781649797278 (Paperback)
ISBN 9781649797285 (ePub e-book)

Library of Congress Control Number: 2022907761

www.austinmacauley.com/us

First Published 2022
Austin Macauley Publishers LLC
40 Wall Street, 33rd Floor, Suite 3302
New York, NY 10005
USA

mail-usa@austinmacauley.com
+1 (646) 5125767

I personally want to thank Austin Macauley Publishers for giving me the opportunity of a lifetime. For taking a chance on an unknown author like myself to help my visions become reality. My gratitude also goes out to Matthew Smith within the accounts department of Austin Macauley for explaining the elements (to my naivety), the publishing setup. Thanks also go out to Jennifer Lane, my production coordinator, for guiding me through the in's, and out's, during the beginning stages of the publishing process during the Covid-19 pandemic and having to do everything online and over the phone. I am very gracious to the beautiful town of Vulcan, Alberta for accepting myself and my children with open arms 14 years ago, giving us a place to call home. I can never forget to recognize my family and close friends that always believed in my overactive and, sometimes, extremely peculiar imagination, that it would either one day make me famous or land me in an institution. Thank goodness it was not the latter.

Chapter One

Even the ceiling was lovely in this delightfully constructed massive house that she and her small family had just moved into. Brynn thought as she lay on her bed staring up, examining the ceiling. It was high and open with large posts and beams crossing overhead in an almost mesmerizing puzzle. Whoever had designed the architecture was an amazing artist with all the combined shapes and designs within the entire house.

Brynn was so exhausted from all the unpacking and establishing order in her new room that she found herself lying on her bed staring up at the ceiling to take a little break. Her family had left the east side of the United States and moved all the way to Canada's farthest western province of British Columbia. It was situated on the coastline of beautiful Vancouver Island. They moved to this magnificent log/post and beam home to start their new lives over in.

Not only was the house majestic but it was surrounded by large cedar trees and nature with a freshwater creek running just behind their backyard and down into the ocean. The backyard was vast and green with a large hot tub and pool sitting just off the large stone patio. This would be a change from the hustle and bustle of the city of New York, especially from Manhattan where she had lived. It was wonderful for her when she could breathe in the fresh crisp air and not feel like she had just inhaled all the exhaust from the cabs flying down Fifth Avenue. Did she miss New York? Nope, not one bit! This move was just what was needed for her and her brother, Sabion. Her mother Jacklyn, however, only did it because they had to.

The house that Brynn and her small family had moved into was far too big for just the three of them. They had lived in a posh penthouse in Manhattan in New York City that looked out over Central Park. With this move, her mother had again purchased something far too extravagant for them. Her mother always had to have the best of the best and it was sometimes embarrassing for Brynn. Her

Mother, Jacklyn, was a Biochemist with a PhD in researching DNA and worked for the government in experiments that she was not allowed to talk about as they were considered classified. Brynn never questioned her mother about her career or what was entailed with it. She respected her mother's explanation that it was classified and that was that. Jacklyn always provided more than everything that was needed for her and Sabion and always had them go to the best private schools, the best private tutors, trainers, and lessons. They always had whatever they needed.

The only thing lacking in Brynn's life was friends. She never knew her father or anything about him. This was a subject that Jacklyn simply refused to discuss with her. She would simply leave the room immediately if any questions about their father arose or where he was or if he were even alive. There was obviously massive amount of emotional pain about their dad where Jacklyn was concerned, so eventually as both her and Sabion grew up, the less and less they asked about their father until it just was not discussed at all anymore. One thing about her mother was when she did not want to talk about anything, no matter how much you pushed or coerced her, she never broke until she decided it was time.

Brynn's thoughts were interrupted with a loud bang coming from her brother's room as he was setting it up and unpacking beside hers. He was still moving his bed into just the right spot that would suit his décor and his newfound appreciation for *feng shui*. Even though he was a skilled champion cage fighter and a fifth-degree black belt in ATA taekwondo, he had an exceptional sense of style with interior decorating. She smiled to herself as she thought of her brother. They had an incredibly special bond that most siblings would never comprehend. They had been close ever since she could remember and even closer now than they had ever been, since they were given no choice but to move out to this beautiful new province to start over.

Brynn inhaled a huge deep breath of fresh air that was coming in from her large open window and then exhaled slowly. This would be a new beginning, a renewed start. She refused to linger in her past life anymore. She had to forget the painful, horrifying memories that were just slowly starting to diminish into a cloudy nightmare from New York. Brynn shook herself of the recollections she refused to let herself think about and slowly dragged herself off her bed to go splash some cool water on her face in the bathroom that connected her and her brother's rooms.

The cool water felt revitalizing as it splashed on her perspiring face, giving her a small amount of renewed energy. She turned to grab a towel only to notice that none of the towels had been unpacked or even put out yet. Searching around the vast bathroom to find something to dry her face on, she came up empty-handed. The bathroom had a large glass standalone shower with multiple showerheads and a Wi-Fi stereo system. She grinned inwardly, thinking how she could not wait to have a long hot shower in the morning with her tunes singing to her as she started her day. The large, jetted tub had nothing near it, so she looked by the toilet and the bidet and giggled a little, not sure when she would ever use the Bidet, as she never had used one before. She was not even sure she knew exactly how one used a bidet but did not want to ask her mom, Jacklyn, and appear ignorant of such a simple contraption to washing your nether regions.

As she stood staring at the bidet with a still-dripping wet face, Sabion entered the bathroom and laughed. "Why are you just standing in the middle of the bathroom dripping-wet?"

She glared over at him and then suddenly jumped towards him, grabbed his shirt, and began drying her face. "Because there are no towels anywhere, so give me the shirt off your back."

Sabion tactfully hurdled himself back into his room. "Oh no, you don't. You're a wet rat. I am wet enough with all the sweating I am doing without you adding to it." She chuckled as she slowly stalked her brother deeper into his room.

They both eyed each other carefully, and then he crouched into a tackle position and without warning dove right at her. He then tossed her none-too-gently onto his bed and then pounced on top of her with his legs straddling on both sides of her hips. This was no easy weight to bear, as he was six feet, four inches tall and weighed a compact two hundred and twenty pounds of rock-solid muscle from his fight training for the last seven years.

Brynn was a mere five-foot-nine and weighed in at only one hundred and twenty-nine pounds of not-so-rock-hard muscle, as she only did yoga and Pilates with her mom. "Get off me, you big oaf. You are too big for me." He just snickered and snuggled his legs even closer to her torso.

"I kind of like this position with you below me and begging. I could get used to this." She struggled and gulped in some air a little more dramatically than needed. She studied her brother's face for a moment, trying to figure out how to get out of this awkward situation, but no ideas were forthcoming.

Sabion had semi-long dark brown wavy hair that caressed his chiseled cheekbones and a sleek strong jawline that he never quite shaved fully and always had a five o'clock shadow. He had deep blue eyes that when angry could turn black and burn holes through your very soul, but when he was in a flirtatious, fun mood, his eyes sparkled a crystal blue, and when in a romantic mood, his eyes could smolder you into a melted pile of womanly hormones. He had full lips and a cleft chin but not so cleft that it was the first thing you noticed on his face. He had beautiful white teeth, even though a few were manmade due to his fighting. Sabion had a little bit of a thicker nose that used to be straight but had been broken more than once from his fighting and now was slightly crooked and wider than it used to be when he was younger. Yes, he was a very gorgeous man of twenty-two years of age and had many women always chasing him at any given time, even though he never seemed to date any of them for exceptionally long.

Sabion was an amazing brother. They were not like your typical brother and sister. It was much more than that. It was more like best friends who could not be apart for more than a day. He always kept her safe from harm, especially where men were concerned. This instantly made her think of her nightmare from New York and the reason that they had moved to this new home in another country across the continent in the first place. Suddenly, she was no longer in a playful mood and asked Sabion in a serious tone to get off her. Sabion started to tickle her on the sides of her breasts by her underarms which usually had her screaming in delight, as that was her tickle spot, but instead Brynn unexpectedly burst into tears.

Sabion instantly removed himself from on top of her, scooped her up into a fetal potion into his arms, positioned her on his lap, and placed his mouth against her hair by her ear, and caressed her arm with his hand. "I am so sorry. Did I hurt you? I am so sorry. I thought you were just kidding me when you said I was too heavy. I would never hurt you on purpose. You know that, right?" He was beside himself with worry, so she trembled a bit, sniffed and inhaled deeply, and tried to control her stupid tears.

"It wasn't you hurting me, Sabe. I just suddenly thought of Mike and…" Sabion became livid with a sudden fueled hatred and held her tighter for a moment. He took a deep breath and steadied his voice before speaking. "That son of a bitch deserved what he got, Brynn. Don't ever forget that. What he did to you was not your fault in any way. You did everything in your power to keep him from bothering you and what happened was his own doing. You hear me? You are not to blame for what happened to that tyrant. I would do it again and will do it again if it means keeping you safe from depraved bastards like that."

"I promised I would protect you for the rest of our lives if I have to. Please do not cry. It rips my soul out when you do." With that, he tilted her face up to his, wiped a tear from the corner of her eye. He tucked a long lock of her hair behind her ear. "I am here for you always and forever; I swear to you." He held her quietly for a few moments and just let her regain her self-control and then sighed and lifted her gently off his lap as if she weighed no more than a child and placed her on the side of his bed and squatted in front of her with his large warm hands resting on the side of her legs. "I want to see your million-dollar smile, or I am going to sit on you again until you either smile and relax or pass out from lack of oxygen from my weight." At this, she lightly smiled a little bit for him.

Sabion always knew how to bring her out of her slumps swiftly. She leaned forward and placed her hands around his neck and squeezed as she slightly shook him playfully back and forth. "You shit, you. How do you put up with me all the time, huh?" Without waiting for an answer, she jumped up and ran out of the room with the excuse that there was more needing to be unpacked before lunch. She quickly disappeared around the bathroom door and into her bedroom as bouncy as she could.

Sabion watched the spot she disappeared from for a while and reflected a little, and then sighing to himself, he got up from the floor out of his crouching position and took himself over to his oversized leather chair by the window and slumped into it. The smell of her was softly wafting up from his shirt and he sighed again, grabbing his shirt and bringing it to his nose. He inhaled deeply. She always smelled like fresh laundry even when she was hot and sweaty. It always amazed him. When he had placed his lips against her hair by her ear, he could smell her fragrance. It was sweet and stimulating like crawling into a newly made bed. It smelled like home; she smelled like home.

Brynn was the most beautiful creature he had ever seen in his entire life. She was not too tall and she was slim, fit yet very curvaceous. Her legs were beautifully shaped and met up with the most definitive hips and derriere a woman could possess. She had long, soft dark brown hair that reminded him of silky dark chocolate and it grew wavy and full hanging three quarters of the way down her sleek, long, and elegant back.

Her stomach was tight, flat, and smooth. She had olive sun-kissed skin and she never needed to tan. Her breasts made his mouth water every time he thought about them. They were perfect in size and shape. They were not too small, and they were not too big. She had a smile and a face that could stop an army. She had high cheekbones with a straight nose, perfect white teeth, and the most voluptuous lips a man could ever imagine kissing. The best part though was her eyes. They were almond-shaped and large, almost too large for a human girl, as they were almost elfin in size and shape. She had long black lashes that never needed any mascara. Her eyes were so dark blue that they were almost violet in color.

Yes, he was her 'brother,' but he had an enormous secret that his mother and he were keeping from Brynn and it was slowly killing him. So many times, he had to catch himself when he was alone with her to not spill everything that he knew. So many times had he caught himself wanting to touch her in ways she would never allow her 'brother' to touch her. If they did not tell her soon, he would defiantly detonate in some horrible fashion that would only end up destroying Brynn and that he would never allow himself to do in any way, shape, or form. Brynn was everything to him. She was even more important than the air he breathed, the food he ate, and the water he drank. She was life itself to him. If she were in his life and by his side, he would do anything in his power to make her happy and keep her safe.

He had a very explosive argument with his mother just before they moved all the way out here. He begged his mother to tell Brynn the truth about everything that he himself had only learned the night of the phone call that started all of this. Their mother only kept repeating, "Not until she felt the time was right." His mother forced a promise out of him, and he agreed very reluctantly. After all, this was for Brynn. He had to keep telling this to himself repeatedly, "For Brynn's sanity," even though it was slaying his.

When they were settled, he would again have the argument about Brynn, and this time he would not take 'no' for an answer or any other excuses that his mother tried to feed him. Brynn would finally know the truth about this secret that his mother had kept from them all these years and then he could actually be able to happily go on with his life with Brynn by his side in a different way than she was now, or so he prayed and hoped. He pushed the negative thoughts out of his head. She would be extremely shocked about the news but hopefully she would be as happy to know the truth finally, as he was, and hopefully, she felt the same for him as he did about her. If she did not, life would not exist for him anymore. He pushed that thought right out of his mind immediately and stood up and began moving his bed again, as it just was not quite right yet.

Meanwhile in Brynn's room, she was feeling a bit ashamed of herself for just bursting out in tears like that. She considered herself extremely strong and resilient. She was always able to bounce back quickly with panache. She had not lost control of her emotions since the 'Mike' incident and never around Sabion. Her tears and emotions seemed to have disturbed Sabion a little more than necessary. The last time she cried was when she thought she would lose him forever when he was nearly sent to jail for life behind bars. *Thank God that never happened,* Brynn thought. She would have lost her rationality if that had ever come into reality. If anything had happened to her brother during the tragedy in New York, then she would have died from heartbreak for sure.

Brynn sat down on her bed and stared out the large window as she wiped a stray tear off her cheek. The ocean scene in front of her was breathtaking, yet Brynn was not really seeing the beauty of it as she stared out in deep thought. Even without her wanting to, she became lost in her thoughts about the nightmare which she promised herself to never dwell on again.

Chapter Two

Brynn had always been an unbelievably beautiful girl, even when she was a baby, according to her mother, Jacklyn. Brynn would always just shake her head when her mother would tell her this. She would ask why she had to go to an 'all girls' school. "Honey," her mom would say, "you are just too young to understand what your looks do to men." Brynn would argue that there were thousands of beautiful girls that went to regular school everywhere, every day, with no issues, so why it was so different for her, as she was just another ordinary girl. Her mother would just sigh and say, "You have never been an ordinary girl, Brynn. Honey, just trust me. Someday, you will understand all of this. Just trust me on this, okay?" That would be it. Her mother would never say anymore even when Brynn would push the matter daily. Nothing ever changed in her mother's argument, so she began to just stop arguing. Sadly, she found out what her mother had been meaning by men not being able to handle her so-called beauty. Brynn did not think it was her looks though. She had just come across a man at just the wrong time that was an absolute irrational lunatic and, for some unexplainable reason, fixated on her.

Several months before Brynn's graduation from high school, Sabion had an especially important fight that would put his name up in lights and start making him a lot of money. If Sabion won this one fight, then he would be on his way to Las Vegas. Brynn never went to his fights anymore because she would end up vomiting in the bathroom of the arena. She could not stand seeing her brother get hurt in any way. Any blood on her brother, even if it wasn't his, (and usually it wasn't), Brynn would instantly be sick, thinking he had been hurt in some very bad way and her stomach would just heave and she would end up running to the bathroom to be sick.

Sabion knew his fighting bothered his sister a lot but begged her to come to this one match, as it was so important to him and his career. He wanted the ones he loved the most to be there cheering him on. He promised Brynn that it would be an extremely quick match, as he studied this competitor's every move and would be able to take him down in only a few minutes. It took Sabion a full week to convince Brynn to come and watch him. The only way he convinced her to come watch was to say he would lose his career-altering match if she did not come, so she finally broke down and agreed to go and watch the match with her mother by her side, of course. When Brynn agreed, he grabbed her in his strong arms and spun her around several times, all the while thanking her and telling her she would not regret it. Unfortunately, they would all end up regretting Brynn's decision to go to the match that night, as this was what started the nightmare for all of them.

Sabion did as he promised and won his match in under two minutes. He had the guy tapping the mat so fast that

Brynn did not even have time to have her stomach twitch in any way. The only blood that she even saw was on the mat and on Sabion's opponent. After the match ended, Sabion came to the lounge where Brynn and Jacklyn were waiting and begged his mother to let him take Brynn to the back and meet all his buddies and fighting mates. He had never done this before, as his mother would never allow it, but since Sabion was so happy with his career-changing win, he asked if he could just this once. Their mother reluctantly allowed it this one time because they would be moving to Las Vegas with Sabion right away due to the win. Jacklyn knew Brynn would be with Sabion and she would be safe if it were quick, so Jacklyn knew no harm would come to her. So, with a "Whoop," he quickly grabbed his sister and literally pulled her in a run to the back to introduce her to all his cage brothers as he called them.

It was hot and smelled like heavy body odor and testosterone in the locker room. There were a lot of fighters milling around and chatting, some waiting for their fighting match and others already done.

Sabion pulled her along excitedly and proudly introduced her to all his mates. A lot of the guys just stared at her with their mouths gaping open when Sabion introduced her to them. Some could not speak, others just stared, and some began to tease him, saying now they understood why he always hid her away at home with Mommy. Brynn did not quite understand what they meant, as she never had any experience with men, so she just smiled at them, which made them gape with jaw-dropped awe even more.

After about fifteen minutes or so, Brynn noticed there was one guy that seemed to hang in the background. He never came forward to talk or to be introduced to her, but he always seemed to be not far from them. Sabion introduced her to his managers and friends but never even tried to introduce her to this man. At one point, he was unnerving her a little with his constant eye contact every time she looked at over at him, so she pointed him out to Sabion, asking, "Who is that?" Her brother looked over at the man Brynn had pointed to and just shrugged, saying that he didn't really know him well yet. He was newer to cage fighting, and since he was only a medium-weight fighter, not a heavy weight fighter, they were not even in the same weight class. They never hung around the same group of fighters, so Sabion explained that they had never been introduced formerly yet. Sabion thought that his name was Mike but was not quite sure, as Mike always kept to himself and was quiet.

After a few more minutes, Sabion turned to Brynn and said, "Let's get out of here. I am starving. Want to have some pizza?" Brynn agreed, so they went back to get their mom and left the coliseum to their favorite pizza restaurant in little Italy.

After that night, Brynn started seeing Mike often. She would see him in the grocery store, at the park, and near her palliates gym, and her yoga building. Brynn never really paid it any attention at first, as she just chalked it up to: 'Once you are introduced to certain things, you begin to see them all the time after that.' She had never been introduced to him before, so her mind must now just be noticing him.

He seemed harmless enough, as he never approached her and never seemed intimidating at all for the first little while.

Brynn started to see him outside her school and following her downtown when she was with her classmates for a school activity. He would always be watching her in the distance to not make anyone else notice him noticing her. He would never look away from her even when she would look directly at him. He would just stand there and watch her. The first mistake Brynn made was not telling her brother or mother about this immediately. The second mistake she made was to try and communicate with Mike. He was quite attractive. He seemed to want to get to know her, so Brynn thought that maybe he was just shy and scared to talk to her. He could also be very intimidated to approach her, since her brother was the number-one heavy weight cage fighter in New York at the moment. She was also always surrounded by either Sabion, her classmates, teachers, her driver, or her mother at any given time. Brynn was never alone; her mother had seen to that for her entire life.

The next time Brynn saw Mike, she was getting out of the limo in front of her school and he was just leaning against the railing to the gated entrance when she decided to smile at him. His response scared her a little as he tilted his head slightly to the side, raised his fist to his mouth, and squeezed his knuckles until they turned white. He never broke eye contact with her the entire time, and he did not return her smile back. Then he just walked away, melting into the crowd.

Brynn shuddered a little and turned away quickly and told herself that she was just imagining things. It would be best to just ignore him from now on, not realizing that smiling at him had been a trigger. Now her sightings of him seemed to escalate. His bravery seemed to escalate as well. Now when she saw him in the crowd, he was a lot closer and not just in the distance. Every so often, she would even find him right next to her at her school field trips like the time at the museum. He was suddenly just

there right behind her, leaning in and smelling her hair and touching the back of her jacket she was wearing. This terrified her but she still did not say anything to anyone, as she felt somehow that she had encouraged him by smiling at him.

Brynn did not have any girlfriends to talk to, as all her classmates avoided her like the plaque. Her female teachers also seemed to just tolerate her but did not want to be around her for more than a few minutes. Her mother always told her it was because they were jealous of her looks and her abilities to be good at anything she had set her mind to. Brynn never understood that. There was nothing special about her looks, as she believed she looked like any other girl at her school. Only Brynn was sadly mistaken, as her appearance was what one would call almost an unearthly beauty. It made women extremely uncomfortable to be around her. Women were extremely jealous of her looks and her figure. She also had a 4.0 grade average and was the topper of her class. Everything Brynn did seemed to come to her naturally without having to try hard. The girls in her school did not want to compete for the attention of people, especially men when Brynn was around. The girls would make snide comments to her to make her feel horrible, so she gave up and stopped trying to make friends at her school. After school, she would just climb into the limo that was sent by her mom to pick her up with a female driver and she would just go home and hang out with Sabion or her mom.

One day, Brynn was leaving the front of the Trump Tower building downtown Manhattan with her class on a school tour when she realized that she had forgotten her sunglasses in the bathroom. With a quick thoughtless decision, she ran back into the building alone before the school shuttle left. When she went into the empty bathroom, she happily found her glasses on the back of the toilet where she had placed them. She quickly tucked them into her bag and turned to leave the stall only to find Mike standing right behind her in the tiny cubical. She almost screamed but her larynx froze as he came towards her slowly and pinned her against the toilet with his body. He deliberately reached out and lightly lifted a lock of her hair away from her chest and brought it up to his nose and drew in a deep breath. He then leaned in towards her. He was not as big as her brother, but he was still exceptionally large, extraordinarily strong, and remarkably much too close to her. Every part of her seized to function; she believed he was going to kill her right there like in the horror movies. She was so stupid to be caught alone in a bathroom with no one there to help her. Nothing on her body would react, not even her lungs. She was sure that she had stopped breathing and that her heart had frozen in mid-beat.

When Mike leaned in, he took another deep breath. He did not touch her with anything except his lips ever so gently on the outer part of her ear. What Mike said was one word, "Soon." It was the most terrifying word that she had ever whispered to her in her entire life. She did not know if she passed out or if he just disappeared out of thin air but suddenly, she was standing alone in the cubicle of the bathroom and he was gone just like that. She had never left a building so fast and her legs wobbled so bad that she was amazed she made it out to the school shuttle without collapsing. As she sat on the shuttle bus back to her school, she began to cry silently and shake uncontrollably to herself, as she had never felt as alone as she did at that very moment, and she only had herself to blame.

What was she thinking smiling at him? Did she make him think that she wanted him to stalk her? Was he stalking her? What the hell was she supposed to do? She had absolutely no experience with this kind of thing. She knew that this was not normal, as naive even as she was with men. Brynn had no idea what it was that men would consider as an invitation. Brynn decided she would never be caught alone again outside of her home. She would always stick by her teachers, her personal drivers, her brother, or her mother wherever she went. This Mike would never catch her alone again, ever. With this decision in place, she began to feel a little bit safer and talked herself into believing that this would eventually make him get bored of his game and he would ultimately leave her alone and lose interest. Sadly, this decision not only made the game much more fun for Mike but it also challenged him to find new methods to get to Brynn in ways that she had never expected.

The very next day after the Trump Tower incident, her cellphone rang. She answered it immediately without checking the caller ID, as the only people that called her were either her mother or her brother. This time, it was neither. Somehow, Mike had gotten a hold of her number and began calling her and would only say one word, "Soon," and then he would hang up. If she did not answer, he would leave it on her voicemail in a gruff whispered voice. He never called her from the same number, so if she blocked that number, he would call her from a different number. Eventually, she only answered her phone if it was her mother or her brother by setting up special ringtones for each of them.

One day, he even called her on her brother's cellphone. He practiced at the same gym as Sabion, so he easily could have snuck a call to Brynn on his phone when he was not looking. He even began messaging that one word, *"Soon,"* on her school email account and once he had somehow left her a note taped to her locker in her secured school where strangers were under no circumstances allowed in at any given time without written permission or an escort from one of the school staff. This note also had one superbly written word on it, *"Soon."*

Brynn still had not told or said anything to anyone about Mike, especially to her mother. Jacklyn was far too overprotective to begin with and would just say, "I told you so," and possibly even take her out of school and make her stay at home and have even less of a life as she had right now. Most of all, she could not tell Sabion. This would send him into a rage, and she did not want him to damage his career in any way, as he was a lethal weapon with just his fists. He could only use his skills in the ring against another trained fighter like himself. If he hit someone in real anger in real life, he could kill them and then he would go to jail and it would be all her fault.

Mike was constantly on Brynn's mind and in her thoughts. She began to stop eating and could not sleep. So much so that she started to lose precious weight and the sparkle left her beautiful eyes and her smile left her lips. Sabion noticed this and began to ask questions. He started to make sure she would eat a little, and he asked her what was wrong constantly to the point that she almost told him on several occasions but would end up fleeing to her room, locking the door, and silently crying to herself instead.

Sabion also started to notice that any little sound or any little movement would have Brynn flinching, or she would begin to shake violently. He noticed too that she would not take her computer or her phone with her anywhere anymore. She even stopped answering any of his phone calls. Her cellphone and laptop would always be left on the table uncharged even when she was in her room or at school.

This went on for a few weeks and Sabion had had enough. He was going to get the truth out of her if it killed him. It was starting to affect his fighting as well. He was always thinking about Brynn and what could be wrong with her. He even lost a few sparing matches with his cage buddies and that was unheard of. His manager began asking questions about what was wrong with him. Was it the pressure of the pending move to Las Vegas that had him rattled? But Sabion did not have any answers for his manager? He was so concerned about Brynn. It was making him sick. He could not concentrate even with his fighting. But how could he tell his manager about this? They would not understand at all. She was beginning to look frail and sickly. This hurt him. Something was not right. She was not talking to him at all anymore, which was the worst part, as she was his best friend and they talked about everything together always.

One night when their mother had gone out of town for the weekend on business, Brynn remembered Sabion literally busted down her door to her bedroom. He demanded to know what the hell the matter with her was. He told Brynn that she had better start talking because he was not leaving until she did. Brynn had been so scared when her door busted in that she could not stop screaming. She thought for sure Mike had come to get her. This startled Sabion so much that he ran to her and just grabbed Brynn and held her tight. He began to cry. He was so concerned about her. Sabion's tears shattered Brynn out of her frantic ear-piercing scream to realize that it was Sabion holding her and not Mike. His tears and his begging her to please tell him what was wrong broke her. She could not see Sabion so disturbed that it had brought him to tears. This large, strong man who was not scared of anything was holding her and begging her to tell him what was wrong as he cried. She had to tell him. She just had to.

When they both calmed down, they sat on the floor of her bedroom and she proceeded to tell him everything. A couple of times, he got up and paced around the room, and then he would sit back down, the whole while not saying a word as he just let her talk and explain to him everything that Mike was doing. His face was red the whole time and he looked like he could kill anything that got in his way, but he still let her talk and never said a word. When Brynn was finally finished telling him everything, he just grabbed her and held her in his arms. Sabion then began apologizing to her, saying how this was his entire fault. He apologized at how he had been so selfish in making her go to his fight. He had begged her to go and that he never should have. On and on he went blaming himself and saying how their mother had been right all along. Suddenly, he just stopped talking, jumped up, and ran from the room.

This was what Brynn had been so afraid of. She knew exactly what he was going to do. He left the penthouse so fast that she could not keep up with him. By the time she had even made it down to the underground parkade, he had already left on his motorcycle and she had no idea where he was going but knew 'who' he was going for. She frantically ran back upstairs to her unlocked penthouse to call her mother to ask for much-needed advice and tell her about what had happened. Now she had to tell her mother everything and get her to call someone to find Sabion before he did something they would all regret. What a mess she had made by not telling anyone much sooner. Now her brother was going to get arrested and it was all her fault. Guilt crept in with a rush of harsh disgust in herself.

There were only two people that she loved more than life itself in this world and she was about to lose one of them to something as stupid as him going to jail for murder. As Brynn ran to the kitchen to grab the landline to call her mother, she failed to see Mike calmly standing in the center of the large living room. She heard the words spoken in a voice a little louder than her heavy breathing. A voice she would never forget. "It's time."

Brynn dropped the phone and spun around. Her worst nightmare had come to life. Not only was her mother out of town but her only protector from this very person standing in her living room had just charged out of the building on his motorcycle to God knew where, looking for him. Here he was, in her home, standing ever so frightening. He looked as if it were Christmas morning and he was about to open a present that he had always wanted. Brynn was all alone, and she was the present. The first thought that hit her was that he had planned the whole thing.

Brynn could not stop herself. This, time her voice did not freeze. She was angry, so angry that she was shaking with it. She was not even scared for herself at the moment; she was scared for Sabion and for the guilt that he would feel about the whole situation if she ended up hurt or even worse, dead.

"What do you want, Mike?" she had said his name with as much venom as she could, and his response was to slowly walk towards her. Brynn noticed that as he came towards her, he kept himself in between the outer door and herself. When he was only an inch from her, Brynn held her ground and did not back away. Mike tilted his head to the side as if he were impressed by her bravado. He then slowly leaned in, ever so slowly to maybe give her time to try to run or panic but Brynn would not give him the satisfaction. Suddenly with finesse, he reached out and picked up a lock of her hair that rested on her right breast and gently placed the hair to his nose and inhaled deeply and then rubbed her lock of hair on his face slowly back and forth. Then he looked Brynn straight in the eyes and stated, "Your scent is mine!"

It was not a question but just a stated fact, almost like he was just talking to himself to confirm something he was already aware of. Mike then leaned in even more and inhaled her hair right on the side of her neck even deeper like the time in the museum and in the bathroom of the Trump building where she had left her sunglasses. Mike leaned back a little, then tilted his head to the left, and looked Brynn in the eyes as his fist came up to his mouth. He squeezed his fist so tight that his knuckles turned white again. He was still holding a lock of her hair in his fist as he did this. The head tilt and the fist clench frightened Brynn so much more than him staring her in her eyes continually and the smelling of her hair. It just seemed crazy. She had witnessed him doing this so many times when she noticed him watching her like he was desperately trying to control himself. Brynn wondered, *If he didn't do this head tilt and fist clench, would it lead to something catastrophic?*

Brynn did not even realize that Mike was slowly leading her into the living room. She did not realize that she was following him subconsciously. He was still holding the lock of her hair in his clenched fist and staring into her eyes as he backed them up towards the large open space to the center of the living room. She was in a trance and did not even know it. Her fear snapped her out of it a little as she was beginning to feel it bubbling up inside of her, to make herself feel brave again and maybe distract him a little. She tried to get him to talk to her. She asked, "What do you want, Mike? Why have you been following me? I don't even know you."

Brynn's bravado quickly started to melt into a cold fear as he said again, "It's time." She had to stall him from whatever he was going to do. Mike just kept leading her to the living room. When he got to the center of the room, he let go of her hair and looked at her up and down. He was not touching her, but his eyes were beginning to look a lot more heated as he looked at her up and down. As they stood there, Brynn thought maybe she could just turn and run up the stairs, lock herself into her room, and call the cops.

Why was he just standing there staring at her? He suddenly shifted his body weight as he leaned in to her again. This took her by surprise, and she flinched. Brynn's flinch made him smile at her and he leaned in even more and took another deep breath by her neck. He slowly leaned back and put the space back in between them but uttered words that shook Brynn to her core. "They are mine and only I will see."

Brynn sucked in her breath. "What the hell did that mean?" Was he sprouting a religious quote or something? Brynn tried to stay calm and took a deep breath before asking Mike, "What is yours?" Mike just tilted his head to the side again but this time, instead of clenching his fist to his mouth, he slowly reached into his hoodie and took out a sharp, wicked-looking knife.

Brynn's eyes widened to the point of watering as the glint of the knife caught her eye. Now she started to panic and now this was getting more terrifying. She was going to die and there was no one there to help her. Brynn's bottom lip started to tremble and she shook her head from side to side and went to step back, away from Mike, but she stifled a scream when Mike gracefully reached the knife out toward her and then as quick as a cat flipped the knife up and under Brynn's tank top and cut one of her shoulder straps apart with a small twist of his wrist. Half her top slipped just above her breast. Brynn grabbed her shirt and tried to back up, but he caught her by her hair and held her fast and looked straight into her eyes. Again, he repeated, "They are mine and only I will see." He never raised his voice, nor did he stop looking into her eyes as he smiled at her like they were the best of friends just having a general conversation. Brynn stated to Mike, hoping this would make him think twice about being here, "My brother should be home any minute, Mike. He will kill you; you know that, right?"

Mike tilted his head to the left and as if he did not even hear her, he slowly and calmly said, "Take…..off…your…clothes." When Brynn just stared at him and did not move, he again raised the knife and cut Brynn's other shoulder strap. It too dropped to just above her breast. Brynn had to use both of her hands now to hold up her shirt to keep from having her breast exposed to this maniac. *Of all the days not to wear a bra. What a stupid thought!* Fear was making Brynn shake slightly. Absolute stupid thoughts were entering her head. Her hands began to sweat. All she could think of now was to beg. "Mike, no, please! Please, Mike, stop this. You do not have to do this. If you leave now, I will not tell anyone. I promise. You can just go and leave. I promise to not say anything to anyone." Mike just stared calmly at her as she begged him. This approach was not working, so Brynn switched tactics. "We can sit and talk and get to know each other?" She knew she was babbling as any minute he could flick that knife and instantly cut her throat open.

Mike responded again with, "It's time."

Brynn looked down at the knife gently hanging in his right hand by his leg. It was as sharp as a Samurai sword;

she knew that with how easily it had cut her shirt straps. Mike stayed very calm and as he stared into her eyes, he flicked up the knife quickly onto the button of her jean shorts. With a quick twitch of the knife, the button popped off as easily as a kid popping off a dandelion's head as they sang, "Mommy had a baby and their head popped off." *What a stupid thing to think of right now!* She could even hear the song in her head as she sang it when she was a little girl playing outside with the dandelions. Mike moved the knife again and caught the tip of it into the zipper of her jeans and in a heartbeat, her shorts were undone. Mike sure knew how to use that knife. She now found herself holding her shorts up with one hand and her shirt with the other. "Mike, please, don't do this. Please, you seem like a nice guy. You don't want to do this." Tears started to well up in her eyes and Mike became blurry as one tear fell down her cheek. Mike leaned forward and licked the tear off her cheek with his tongue as Brynn stood frozen in utter fear. Mike licked his lips and moaned lightly as he leaned back and gave her a slight smile. Slowly, Mike stated again, "Take…off…your…clothes."

The words were sobbed out of her throat, "Mike… I can't."

Mike tilted his head to the left again as he still stared into her eyes. "When you say my name, it makes it right. My name belongs on your lips, Brynn." The eye contact was becoming almost unbearable. He was licking his lips and starting to breathe a little heavier and his eyes were as black as coal and seemed to burn a hole into her soul.

Mike's eyes seemed more dangerous than the knife he was holding. They held crazy calmness and she could not look away from his penetrating stare. Without much movement, Mike lifted the knife again and lightly dragged the back of it across her hand that was holding her shirt. She wasn't cut but the cold steel startled her enough that she let go of her shirt, and with a movement as quick as a cheetah, he had the knife up and under her shirt and quickly cut it open and it fell to the floor without even leaving a mark on her skin.

He was incredibly good with this knife as if he trained with it or it was an extension of him. For a split-second, she stood stunned with her breasts proudly pouting in his direction. This seemed to be his undoing. His calm exterior snapped as he dropped his gaze to the sight of her perfect breasts. Mike let out a terrible moan and came forward until he was only an inch from her. He raised one hand up and mimed his hand, rubbing her nipple with his palm without touching her. His breath came even sharper and she could feel the hotness of it. She began to shiver, and this made her nipples stand at attention and pucker into beautiful peaks and he moaned again. He just stood and stared at her breasts as if he were mesmerized by them. Her breath was coming short as he stared at her breast moving up and down. With him still staring at her exposed breast, he said, "Better than perfect, better than I pictured in my mind. So much beauty. So much for me." He blinked a few times and leaned his head back and licked his lips.

Brynn looked down at the knife. Since he seemed so distracted with her breasts, maybe she could kick the knife out of his hand and run screaming out the front door. Brynn's thoughts were interrupted as he began speaking again. "When our son is born and your breasts are full of milk, I will partake too. I will drink from them." Brynn had enough. This made her almost vomit in her mouth but at least he did not mean to kill her if he was talking about them having a child together. Without much thought, Brynn kicked out hard and fast, hitting the knife out of Mike's hand, or so she thought because as soon as she raced by him, he had a hold of her in a very firm grip and suddenly she was on the floor, being pulled under him. In a second, he was on top of her, smelling her breasts, her throat, and her hair.

He seemed like he could not get enough of her scent into him and he was becoming frantic. Somehow, the knife was back in his hand and he held it now to her throat. "Don't make me hurt you, Brynn. My body entering your body will happen, you, me, mine always, now and forever," Mike stated as his one hand hovered on top of her breast. Still he did not touch her, and his legs straddled each side of her hips tightly. His gaze felt almost worshipping as he looked at her half naked body lying beneath him. He began to moan as he leaned down and smelled her again. Brynn's heart was racing a mile a minute.

He was saying crazy things. He was going to rape her and then he was going to slit her throat and there was nothing she could do about it. Almost as if he read her mind, he leaned to her ear. "You are mine; I control you now." Mike leaned back but changed his mind and grabbed her by the throat, gently turning her head and whispering, "You are everything to me." He said it almost in an apologetic manner as he leaned back and lifted himself slightly off her lap to cut open her shorts. Soon, Mike had her shorts cut off and he threw them away off to the side. He sat back and looked away from her eyes for the first time in a few minutes and looked down at her shivering naked body. His breath caught in his throat. "Perfect." He still had a hold of her throat with one hand and placed the knife down with the other. He started to fumble with his pants and Brynn realized that right now may be her only chance to escape.

In a flash, she grabbed for the knife and when she felt it in her hand, she slashed it at his face. The knife hit his cheek but only on the dull side. She did hit him hard enough though and he rolled off her. This was enough for her to wiggle out from under him. Before she could scramble away from him, he grabbed her from behind and laughed. He was not too gentle this time as he threw her back under him. Brynn's attacking Mike seemed to fuel his desire on. She slapped him, rose, and screamed with all her might into his face, but he was so strong, and he had somehow grabbed the knife away from her again. She could feel his swollen large hardness against her leg now. Her fighting him had aroused him even more. Next, her panties were gone in a flash. She was now totally naked under his body. Somehow, his shirt had been taken off and she could see that he was solid rock-hard muscle from his cage fighting.

Brynn bounced and bucked under him, trying to get him off. He was somehow holding her and taking off his pants with his other hand with no trouble at all. She could not let him take her like this. She had never known a man's touch, and this would not be the way she would have her first experience. She raised herself up and screamed in his face and began to scratch at his eyes. This startled him a little and he shifted his weight. Brynn closed her eyes and began to twist and turn with all her might. She would die before he raped her. He would never get her this way.

She could feel his hard, throbbing member against her thigh now and his fullness was so close to where it soon would all be over, and he would be tearing inside of her if she did not think fast. She squeezed her eyes shut and screamed for him to get off her when she heard a deep animalistic roar. Suddenly, Mike was lying very heavily on top of her. This scared her to her core, thinking she had pushed him too far and now he was going to really hurt her. Was he preparing to enter her? Or worse, was he now going to kill her?

Out of nowhere, his weight was suddenly completely off her. She was free. Without looking back, she instantly turned and crawled away screaming, thinking he had gotten off her to take his pants off fully. She began to claw her way up the stairs when she could hear moaning, grunting, pounding, and then a wet splatting sound. Suddenly, there was a loud crunch, more gurgling, and then nothing.

The sound was not natural. It sounded like a bear was behind her. She should have just run but she looked behind her as she half crawled and half staggered up the stairs. There in a fury of rage was Sabion. He had Mike on the floor and Mike did not have a chance. Sabion had already smashed his face in and there was blood everywhere. Mike's face was gone. Sabion had totally smashed his face into the back of his head. Sabion was still smashing at a face that was no longer there. This all happened in a fraction of a second.

Brynn came to her senses immediately. She flew down the stairs and jumped on Sabion's back, all the while screaming at him to stop. Only when she screamed that he was dead several times did Sabion snap out of it. Panting, Sabion flew around and grabbed Brynn. "Did he hurt you? Did he touch you? Did he, oh God, did he…" Sabion could not finish as he looked at Brynn and inspected every inch of her skin to make sure there was nothing hurt, cut, or bruised.

"Sabion, he didn't. You stopped him before he could hurt me." Sabion looked at Brynn in the eye and then grabbed her fiercely and hugged her like he would never let her go.

"I am so sorry, Brynn; this was my entire fault. He was waiting. He knew. He knew I was going to confront you tonight. He heard me talking to my manager earlier on today at the gym because he kept harassing me till I told him what was bothering me. He said it would make me feel better and maybe get me to concentrate better on my fighting again. So, I thought about it and I broke down. I told him everything and then told him what I was going to do to get the information out of you and to find out why you were so scared. Mike was there. He heard everything. He knew once I found out about him, I would go looking for him once you confessed. He knew you would be alone. Oh my God, Brynn! I let him touch you. I led him right here to you. A buddy of mine said he saw Mike lurking around the corner listening as I talked to my manager, but at the time, he did not think anything of it until tonight when I showed up looking for him. When I found out that he had heard everything, I was saying to my manager I knew he would be here; I could not get here fast enough. I am so sorry."

Brynn and Sabion just held each other as he confessed. All the while, Brynn was repeating, "No, Sabion, it is my fault, Sabion." Then they both just cried and held each other as the body of Mike lay bleeding out beside them on the penthouse's living-room floor.

Chapter Three

Brynn shivered as she went over the memories that she tried so hard to suppress about Mike. It was almost the most terrifying memory she had ever endured but there was an even worse memory as things developed over the next few days after Mike's death. Brynn almost lost her brother to jail for murder. Her mother had flown back as soon as she found out what happened, and everything whirled into a blur.

The NYPD swarmed into the penthouse after the neighbors had called about a possible domestic disturbance with all the screaming and wailing that had happened during Brynn's attack and as Sabion and Mike's struggle had been heard by the floor below and the other penthouse at the top of their tower. The police asked question after question as they all sat around Mike's corpse while forensics did their investigation, and the coroners came and left after they pronounced Mike's time of death and then removed the body. The police had separated Sabion and Brynn for questioning. The questioning soon became a disaster as they had to have male cops question Sabion, as the female cops couldn't keep their wits about them as they tried to question the most handsome man they had ever met and the same happened with Brynn's questioning. They had to have only the female officers question Brynn, as the male officers were having the same problem questioning the most alluring woman they had all ever met in their lives as well.

At the end of all the questioning, they had Sabion in handcuffs and they were leading him out of the penthouse to go to the precinct for the night. They had to take Brynn to the hospital as she was not allowed to stay in the penthouse because the investigation was taking place there and they had to make sure she was mentally and physically okay after the attack on her. Brynn demanded to see Sabion, but she was kept from him as he was from her. She begged the officers for her to just say goodbye, but they were having nothing to do with any of it. The female officers were quite rude to Brynn, as they suspected that this was all her fault. They had already made the assumption that somehow she had something to do with all of this and they were feeling bad for Sabion for his protection of Brynn, as now they felt he would be sentenced to life in prison for murder because of her.

The officers were extremely disturbed with all their reactions to both Sabion and Brynn and they all wanted to get out of the penthouse and get this case wrapped up, especially since Sabion was a champion cage fighter and a lot of the officers were fans of his. This was going to be a very publicized case; this always made the police uncomfortable. The police did not want to make any mistakes or have even a hair out of place for the public to think they were not doing their jobs properly.

Brynn had suffered one of the worst nights of her life. She was terrified for Sabion and what would happen to him.

She was distracted to the point of a mental breakdown and all she could do was cry. The doctor finally gave her a heavy sedative and they made the officers leave her alone for the night, stating that she needed her rest. They could come back the next day for questioning. They all left but they kept a police officer at her door. Soon, Brynn was asleep from the medication and the hospital floor settled down for the night.

Sabion paced back and forth in the cell. They had to give him a private cell soon after he was placed in the common cell, as some of the other gang related inmates had tried to test Sabion's fighting skills by surrounding and attacking him. Sabion held his own against four inmates very well until the guards came running in. They had to remove him from the common cell for the other inmates' safety, as all the four men were looking worse for wares as Sabion had attacked them like a grizzly bear. Sabion was so angry that he could have easily killed all of them. He was desperately worried about Brynn and constantly asked the officers how she was and where they had taken her, but they would not answer him. As he paced back and forth like a caged lion, he blamed himself over and over about what had happened. He began to talk himself into accepting his fate. He began to believe that maybe he did deserve to be in jail for forcing Brynn to go to his fight. None of this would have happened if he had just let his pride go. If he had just not wanted to show off to Brynn, then this would have never happened.

Sabion was so furious with himself. He began to punch a wall and hit it so hard that he broke his hand in several places. The cops were so scared of him that they had a doctor come in and sedate him at gunpoint as they patched his hand up. They decided to keep him on suicide watch for the night as well. The sedative did not make him sleep, even though they gave him a dose that should have put a small horse under. His adrenaline was running so high that all it did was calm him down enough that the doctor could cast his hand. After his hand was all fixed up and he came out of the sedative, he began to pace again but remained calm as the officers watched his every move now. They said if he acted up again, they threatened to handcuff him by his wrists and ankles and put him in a straitjacket if necessary.

All Sabion could think about was Brynn. 'Is she okay? Is she afraid? Is she safe? Did Mike rape her? Did I get there in time? Is she too afraid to tell me if Mike had raped her?' These questions kept running through his mind repeatedly. The pain meds were beginning to wear off and Sabion relished it, as it made him concentrate on the pain a little instead of Brynn. He was not concerned at all for himself. He would do it again and smash that bastard's face in over and over if given a chance. When he rushed into the penthouse and saw Mike pinning Brynn to the floor with his pants around his knees and her naked under him, screaming and begging for him to stop, he just lost it.

Rage hit him once more and the pain in his hand did not even faze him anymore as the image of Mike on top of Brynn and touching her without her permission dominated his thoughts. Yep, he would relish in killing that bastard every day of his life for what he did. If he by some miracle got out of jail, no one would ever hurt Brynn again if he had anything to do with it. She would be by his side for the remainder of her days if that was what it took to keep her safe.

Chapter Four

When the trial began, it was a debacle in the media. The papers and the news had it so sensationalized that Brynn and her mother, Jacklyn, could not even leave the penthouse after a while. All the reporters and spectators milling around the streets just waiting to get a photo or a quick comment kept them isolated and not able to go out. The news had named the horrible event as 'beauty and the obsessed fighter.' Some reporters even stated that it was Brynn's fault due to how beautiful she was and that they even slightly understood how someone could become that obsessed with her. This made Brynn so upset and angry. She could not even watch or read the news anymore. How dared they blame her looks for the way Mike had stalked her and almost raped and killed her! She was just a woman that had been completely terrorized by a madman. She did not do anything wrong and she did not deserve what he tried to do to her because she was supposedly pretty.

Brynn looked out one of the penthouse windows to see the street below. She was able to see protesters for women's rights and protesters for women against violence, reporters, news vans, cameras, and people who just wanted to see what was going on. They were jammed in the street below their building and police had to redirect traffic for heaven's sake. People were everywhere. It made her sick that the city of New York acted like this about the case. If Sabion had not been the number-one cage fighter in the state right now, then none of this would have been such a media frenzy.

Brynn was so worried about the trial. She was even more worried about Sabion. She was not able to see him or even talk to him on the phone in case they were able to collaborate a story. Brynn had never felt so alone in her life. Her brother, protector, and best friend was locked in a prison awaiting trial for murder and all she got was his letters given to her by her mother. Jacklyn could go see Sabion and she did so every day. That was the best part of Brynn's day lately when her mom would come back from visiting Sabion and hand her a letter from him. She absorbed every word from every letter, even though she knew that the guards had read it before they allowed it out of the prison. She would snatch the letter when her mother gave them to her and quickly run to her room to read it in privacy and cry.

Brynn was also fighting a lot with her mom. Jacklyn would tell Brynn over and over that she should have told them about what was happening with Mike immediately. Then none of this would have happened. Jacklyn blamed Brynn and stated that she should have kept her in home schooling and should have had a tutor, as she knew that one day this would happen. When Brynn would question her about why she knew that this was going to happen and ask her to explain. Jacklyn would just state, "I told you so," then clam up, and walk away.

The next month felt like an eternity and yet swept by within moments awaiting the trial date. Brynn had missed her graduation and her prom but that did not bother her in the least. She did graduate with honors and that was really all that mattered to Brynn anyways. She did not have any friends at school, and she was going to have Sabion take her to her prom as her date, since she did not know any boys. She could not face walking across the stage with her brother sitting in a jail cell anyways. It just would not be right without him. It was just another day that passed so fast with the upcoming trial that Brynn almost forgot. All she could think about was her testimony and how she could get her brother out of jail. Brynn was allowed to go to the trial but only as a witness on the witness stand.

Brynn was so nervous. The cameras were allowed in the courtroom, even though her mother had fought ridiculously hard to keep them out. The courtroom was always packed with people with standing room only. The court grounds were full of everyone just trying to get a glimpse at the so-called 'beauty' and the 'gorgeous, famous fighter' that was a killer. A bunch of women had formed a 'Free Sabion from prison' fan group and there were at least two hundred of them all over the courthouse lawn and street with his pictures plastered all over their banners and picket signs. Some of the signs said, *"Sabion, would you kill for me?"*

"Sabion, will you marry me?"
"Sabion, I want your baby!"

This all made Brynn terribly upset.

Their private lives were in tatters and one of the two people she loved dearly may be about to go to jail for murder and the city's courtroom was like a movie set. The stress was so intense for her that she had to keep her sanity by just remembering that she would be able to see Sabion for the first time in over a month in the courtroom. It was a horrible way to be able to see him but at least she could lay her eyes on him personally and see if he were okay for herself.

The day of court arrived, and Brynn found herself unable to contain her nerves. She dressed conservatively but professionally and wore light makeup. She did not want to draw any more attention to herself than there already was. It was still bound to happen no matter what she wore or looked like. She was the 'beauty' in this case that had been sensationalized by the media and she was the flavor of the moment. She put a hoodie over her demure white pant suit and covered her face as they pulled up to the courthouse. Her mother was just as nervous but would not give more than one-word answers to Brynn's questions. This was so unlike her mother. Yes, they had been fighting constantly for the last month, but her mother was usually very outspoken and tough. She seemed like a shadow of herself lately. Brynn knew her mother was just as worried about Sabion as she was but something else was bothering her mother. When questioned, Jacklyn would only shrug or state, "She was just worried about Sabion."

Brynn knew her mother was lying. About what, she could not put her finger on it. Her mother had been locking herself in her home office for a long time every day but only gave the excuse that she had to work in home office instead of at the lab with all the attention that was going on with the media and the trial. This made sense but Brynn felt it was much more than what her mother was telling her. Brynn had to stop wondering as they neared the courthouse and took in a very deep breath. *Just one quick walk into the courthouse.* Brynn would keep her hoodie up and her head down and just march in behind the security guards her mother had hired for this day. It was her day of testimony, her day of regurgitating everything that 'Mike' had done to her, leading up to the attack and his death. Her lawyers had prepped her for everything that may be thrown at her by the crown.

This was Sabion's life that was in jeopardy. She would never forgive herself if he did not get the jury to find him 'not guilty.' Sabion's plea was 'justifiable homicide' but the crown wanted him to go to jail for the brutality of the homicide, since Mike's face had been totally decimated and his skull caved in as well. They wanted him to go to jail for, at the minimum, 'manslaughter.' This was a reduced sentence if he were found guilty, but he could still go to jail for five to ten years and that just could not happen. Brynn would just die of heartbreak. Brynn's mom, Jacklyn, leaned forward in her seat and tapped her on her knee. "Honey, it's time. Just follow the security guards and do not stop, do not answer any questions, and keep your head down. Don't let the media get a picture of your face like they did the first week of this trial that caused everyone to go into a crazy frenzy with all of this." Brynn cringed but held her tongue.

Brynn had never had her photo out in the public before or in the paper and on the news. Somehow, when she was on the penthouse balcony's rooftop a few days after being released from the hospital after the attack, she decided to get some air. She could not go out on the street, so she decided to go out on the balcony to take in the scenery of

New York. She leaned up on the railing with the wind in her hair as a helicopter flew past with a guy leaning out of the side with a large camera. Little did Brynn know that it had been a reporter just waiting for her to come outside. She had thought she was safe at the top of her penthouse balcony but did not realize the lengths the media would go to get a snapshot of her.

The very next day, all hell broke loose. The newspapers and the morning news reports had her picture all over the TV and tabloids. There she was, leaning over the railing looking out at the skyline with an oversized sweater wrapped around her body and her hair blowing in the wind. It looked like she had posed for the photo. Even she had to admit it was a nice photo but the media then began calling the case 'beauty and the obsessed fighter' and all of the sudden, the whole case turned out to be about her beauty and no longer about the brutality of the attack and the case of her poor brother in jail for possible murder.

Her mother, Jacklyn, was so mad at her when she saw the newspapers and the news. She was actually frantic about her daughter being caught in a photo and now it was on the front page of all the papers and on every news station across the state and maybe even the country due to the celebrity status of Sabion and now her face. At first, Brynn felt terrible about the photo and she was no longer allowed outside, nor without a hoodie over her head and a scarf around her face. Brynn began to wonder why it was so important to stay under the radar for a photo so badly. What did it matter? It seemed her mother was angrier at the photo of Brynn than she was about the attack, the trial, and that Sabion was in jail. This just did not make sense to Brynn. It confused Brynn and made her feel dirty and cheap. What was wrong with one lousy photo? Jacklyn would not let her forget about it either. Maybe this was just a way her mother was able to handle her grief about the situation by fixating on the photo thing. Brynn just did not know.

Her mother began to get out of the car as the door was opened by the driver and the crowd pushed forward. The questions began to be shouted. It was chaos. Brynn was almost pushed back into the car until the security guards got a hold of the crowd and managed to get them to partially back away. There were cops involved with the crowd control as well. Brynn was overwhelmed. It was not as if she was Lady Gaga or Beyoncé. She was just a girl who happened to be the sister of the best cage fighter in the state at this moment, who had been stalked and attacked by a madman who also happened to be a fighter. What made this into such a ridiculous sensation that everyone wanted to see her and hear about the trial? Were people that bored?

She was diligent in keeping her head down and not looking up. She even managed to keep her hoodie on and her hair hanging in front of her face as she was quickly ushered into the building. Once the doors closed and they were in a witness room, she could still hear the crowd outside as if they were in the next room. She sighed at some relief though. Part One of this day was over and now, she had to focus on giving the most graphic horrible details she could muster without vomiting on the stand to save her brother from a manslaughter conviction.

Brynn's lawyers came in and went over a few more things and gave her a pep talk and reminded her again that this was her brother's life that was in her hands which she did not appreciate, but she knew that they were right. After waiting in the room for about an hour, the door finally opened, and she was escorted into the courtroom.

Chapter Five

When Brynn entered the courtroom, there were gasps and whispers. Brynn did not care about them. All she wanted to do was immediately find Sabion and that was what she did. She found him in an instant. They locked eyes and Brynn instantly teared up. Sabion made to stand up but his lawyer put a hand on his arm and made him sit back down and whispered something to him. Sabion never lost eye contact with Brynn as she was led to the witness stand. She was so relieved to see him looking healthy and he had a large, beautiful smile on his face just for her to show her that he was okay and as happy to see her as she was at seeing him. She smiled back at him and almost tripped as she entered the witness stand, which made Sabion chuckle. When she was finally seated, she still could not take her eyes from Sabion, which gave her strength and calmed her slightly.

She would tell her story to the best of her ability to get her brother free. When the courtroom, judge, and jury heard about how that maniac had stalked her, threatened her, and then attacked her, there was no way that he would be sentenced with manslaughter. Her truth and her passion to free her brother would not fall on deaf ears. At this thought, she broke eye contact with Sabion for just a few seconds to look at the jury. This made her even happier as more than half the jury was women, and they all were looking at Sabion like they wanted to eat him for dessert.

This was wonderful for Sabion even if it was not really his peers sitting in the jury section. They looked like they all wanted to marry him. Brynn smiled to herself and then looked over at Sabion once more and smiled warmly at him. There were some gasps again and more whispers to the point that the judge had to ask everyone to be silent. All Brynn did was smile. *Why did this cause such a disturbance?* She looked over at Sabion again and he just nodded and raised his eyebrows at her.

After Brynn laid her hand on the Bible and swore to tell the whole truth and nothing but the truth, so help her God, she was instantly asked by Sabion's lawyer to give her testimony by starting from the very beginning and to recount as much detail as she could remember in her own words.

Brynn swallowed hard. No one had heard the whole story, except for Sabion, about the stalking and what Mike had done to her with his calls and notes, accosting her in the bathroom and showing up at her school etc. Brynn knew though that even Sabion had not heard the attack details from the night that Mike had caught her in her home alone. She closed her eyes and took in a deep breath. She had to hold back the tears. She could not cry right away. She had to tell her side of the story audibly without blubbering so the jury could not hear what she had to say. She had to be strong and not be a victim. She knew this would mentally kill Sabion all over again to hear her account of the actual attack, but it had to be told for his sake.

While Brynn recounted all the gory details, Sabion sat quietly until she started to tell the court what happened the night of the attack and what Mike had physically done and said to her. Sabion started to shift in his seat uncomfortably, run his hands through his hair, stretch his neck back and forth, clenching his jaw. This was torture for him, and she could see that he was 'again' blaming himself for it all. Sabion's face was getting redder by the minute. It looked like he was about to explode with rage. When Brynn explained how he cut off her clothing and was on top of her, trying to get his pants off, Sabion slammed his fist on the table he was sitting behind and cursed. This startled the entire courtroom as papers flew everywhere from the lawyer's pile on the table to the courtroom floor. He was so angry that he had sweat glistening on his forehead and it looked like he was fighting back an explosion. The jurors noted how upset this account was making Sabion and this was a good thing, or so Brynn hoped.

The judge gave him a stern, "Calm yourself, young man, or we will remove you from the court and find you in contempt," but everyone could see even the judge was upset by the testimony and details of the attack that Brynn had given. You could see the jury sitting with their mouth agape, trying not to look upset and moved by the testimony, as they were not supposed to show any emotion. Even the audience in the courtroom was straining to hear every word and shaking their heads over Brynn's recount of the attack. Brynn was counting on this reaction and then explained what had happened when her brother showed up during the attack. Brynn stressed how he had thrown Mike off her as he was trying to rape her and how he had saved her from definite rape and possible death at the hands of her attacker. The ladies in the jury all sighed as they visualized Sabion saving the damsel in distress. Then Brynn told the court that she didn't even think Mike knew what hit him, as it was over in just minutes with her attacker lying dead on the floor by the bar and Sabion and her sobbing into each other's arms and how he was so sorry he let this madman hurt her. Again, all the ladies in the jury and courtroom sighed and the men all nodded in an approving manner.

Brynn's mother was crying. Brynn had never seen her mother cry before. Sabion was even trying to hold back the tears and failing miserably. He mouthed to Brynn, "I'm sorry," and Brynn mouthed back to Sabion,

"I'm sorry too."

After Brynn's testimony ended, she was asked to step down from the witness booth and to go back to sit with her mother at the front pew, just behind Sabion. He watched her the whole way and Brynn sat right behind him. They both wanted nothing more than to huge each other but knew the time would come soon and held back so as not to get caught with contempt of court. Sabion's lawyers also entered some other pieces of evidence that her stalker Mike had made. As the court listened to the explanation of what one of the pieces of evidence was, the lawyers brought out a tape that Mike had constructed.

This tape entailed recorded splicing of phone conversations that Brynn had made in her own home over many phone conversations that Mike had recorded of

Brynn's private phone calls. Brynn had no idea about this tape until this moment in court and was furious as well as her mother, Jacklyn. Jacklyn had paid a hefty price for their penthouse due to the supposed security of the building and was visibly upset that somehow Mike had paid off a maintenance man at the building and was able to tap into and tape their private phone conversations. Mike manipulated conversations that Brynn had had with her brother and mother and made a tape edited to sound like she was talking to Mike about sexual things. If Brynn had not been so disgusted and informed about how the tape was made and edited, she would have believed she had physically said these things to Mike, and he had just taped them. All the court could hear Brynn's voice over the speakers as the lawyers pressed 'play.'

"Oh, how I want you to come, oh yeah, just like that. Touch me right there. I love you. You are everything to me. Michael! Yes! Yes! Please touch me. Michael, you are my life! Kiss me. I am coming! You are so big! So strong. Love me! I love you, Michael. I am yours."

How many conversations did he have to piece together to get this all spliced so seamlessly? How many hours did he spend to get it to sound just like she was talking to him while they were having sex and all he did was record it? Shivers went down her spine as she listened, and she was getting sick to her stomach. The Michael she was actually talking about was their chef that came in to cook for them through the week and her mother and she would always discuss what they would want him to put on the menu for the next week or so. The 'I love you' was her talking to either her mom or to Sabion and all the other stuff was words picked out from conversations here and there and brilliantly spliced together to make it sound like a heated sexual conversation that Brynn just spoke naturally. This upset Sabion as well. He was red in the face again and Brynn could tell he was fantasizing about killing Mike all over again.

The other evidence was photos of Brynn. There were dozens of them. They had found them in Mike's apartment in a collage on his wall. They were of her at school, getting out of her limo, going to her yoga class, her in some complicated yoga and Pilates poses, and her on the Shuttle bus and walking with her classmates for school tours. Some of the photos had writing on them stating, *"Soon," "she is mine,"* and *"I must have her."* All of this was a good thing, Brynn guessed, as it showed how obsessed he was with her and the jury could see this as well. It disturbed her more than she could say, as she was so oblivious to all of it at the time that he was taking these pictures of her and she never knew. Her life was not her own and he ripped her soul out by all of this. She was never so glad that he was dead as she was sitting in the courtroom and seeing all Mike had done in his obsession with her.

After Brynn's testimony, photos, and the tape, it was now the crown's attempt to try and convince the court and the jury of Sabion being guilty of manslaughter. They knew they had to try and get the jury back on their side, but you could see after her testimony and the tape that Mike had spliced, and all the invasive photos of Brynn's daily life they knew that it was a lost cause. They too were brothers and parents of daughters. You could see them all thinking that they would have done the same exact thing as Sabion did at the moment if it had been them. They halfheartedly tried to convince the jury that even though he saved his sister from a sinister fate, this was still an over kill. That it was a brutal attack that left a man dead, but the crown had no real luster for a manslaughter conviction anymore.

As they sat in the courtroom, Brynn's mother took her hand in hers and leaned towards her and whispered, "Brynn, thank you for being so strong. I love you and I am so sorry I have been so hard on you this last month. I never knew how bad it was." Brynn squeezed her mother's hand and smiled softly at her. Brynn breathed a large sigh of relief. Her mom was back. Soon, the jury would come back with a not-guilty verdict and this nightmare would all be over.

As Brynn had been the last witness in the trial, the judge talked to the jury and asked them to retreat into the jury room and to please remember their vows and to deliberate together to come up with a verdict. The judge dismissed the court until the jury came back with a verdict and the court would be adjourned till then.

Brynn stood up and quickly leaned over the barrier and grabbed Sabion with all her might in an over-the-railing hug. Sabion took advantage of it as well before the bailiff came over to take him back to jail. They kissed each other on the cheek and quickly squeezed each other's hands. The bailiff came over and pulled Sabion away and gave him an angry glare, even though you could see he much admired the young man standing before him and took him out quickly. The volume in the courtroom was suddenly getting very loud and people were starting to try and crowd Brynn and her mother to ask questions. This was Brynn's cue to get the heck out. Jacklyn and Brynn were ushered out of the courthouse and were placed in the limo parked at the back of the courthouse. They did not want the pressure of the media to start again as it had that morning. Some reporters tried to get to them though as they quickly snuck around the side of the courthouse, but security stopped them immediately as they started screaming out questions to Brynn.

Both Brynn and Jacklyn breathed a large sigh of relief at the same time as they settled into the limo with the door shut behind them. Jacklyn looked at Brynn and grabbed her hand again and moved to sit beside her. All she said was, "I am proud of you. You did really good up there today. I am so sorry." The rest of the way, Brynn just snuggled into her mother's side and they rode home in silence.

Chapter Six

"We, the jury, find the defendant not-guilty." Brynn almost fainted. She was so relieved upon hearing the jury member read the verdict. It had only taken the jurors three hours of deliberation to come up with a not-guilty verdict. It was only the next day they were all called back to the courtroom to hear the verdict announced. Sabion stood up and was getting pats on the back from his lawyers and everyone suddenly exploded with clapping, hoots, and hollers from all the people packed in the courtroom. Everyone was eager for a not-guilty verdict. Everyone was now calling Sabion a hero. Even the papers had stated this, as he had gotten one crazy lunatic off the streets and saved his sister from a horrible assault and possible death. No one wanted to see Sabion go to jail. Even the crown prosecutor came over and shook Sabion's hand and the judge was nodding and smiling as well. Sabion turned around and gave Brynn the biggest, happiest smile and gave a big thumbs-up sign. This was the best day ever for their family. Sabion was not guilty of murder and he would be released as soon as the paperwork could be finished within the hour. Brynn could not wait to hug her brother and just have him back at home with her.

After the almost impossible time of trying to get out of the courthouse with Sabion answering reporters' questions, signing autographs, and fighting off the thralls of women waiting to get a glimpse of him, Brynn was whisked away into the limo, which was fine with her and waited patiently. It was extremely late when they returned home. Brynn was exhausted but just could not stop staring at Sabion and holding his hand as they sat beside each other on the drive home. Now sitting in the penthouse's living room with her head rested on his shoulder, she listened to him breathe and they all sat in a stunned yet happy silence. Brynn was almost asleep resting on Sabion's shoulder, curled up beside him when the phone rang. Jacklyn stood up from her lounger across from them, frustrated and grumbled about who could be calling this late in the evening and went to answer the phone.

Immediately after answering the phone, Jacklyn hissed to the person on the other line to hold and she would take the call in her office. Jacklyn soon disappeared and this was Brynn's cue to take herself off to bed, as this was probably her mother's work calling, as sometimes, they did this late at night. Sabion looked happy but extremely exhausted as well from the day's events and without a word, like an unspoken telepathic communication, they both stood up and went upstairs hand in hand. Without a question, Brynn followed Sabion into his bedroom. She crawled into Sabion's bed, as she just could not stand being away from him for even a moment, since he had been in jail over the last month. She was almost afraid it was a dream, and she would wake up and he would be gone. Without question,

Sabion crawled in beside her and just hugged her to him. They fell asleep almost immediately.

Suddenly, there was yelling and lights turning on and doors slamming. Was Brynn having a bad dream? What the heck was going on? Jacklyn was grabbing at both Sabion and Brynn, shaking them awake and yelling at them to get up and something to the likes of they were leaving right now, and they must get out of New York. The past had finally caught up with them and they were in danger. Jacklyn was frightened as well as steaming mad. When Brynn and Sabion sat up and just stared at their mother in utter confusion and exhaustion, Jacklyn became even more frustrated. "Didn't you hear me? We are leaving and we are leaving right now. Get up! Pack your bags quickly. We have to go."

Sabion was the first to respond to his mother's lunatic ranting and got up, stating, "Mom, calm down. Let's go downstairs and work this out." He put his arm around Jacklyn's shoulder and led her out of the room and back downstairs. When they reached the kitchen, he opened a bottle of wine and poured his mother a glass and handed it to her. Jacklyn would not sit down though, as she ignored the glass of wine and began pacing. Brynn had come down the stairs and was staring at her mother as if she had suddenly grown two heads. Something had scared her mother and Brynn was now becoming worried, very worried.

"Mom, they can't revert a not-guilty verdict, can they? Is this why we must leave? Are they coming to take Sabion away, Mom? Is he going back to jail?"

Jacklyn stopped pacing and stared at the two of them as she snapped out of her panic. She suddenly realized what she had just done. How was she going to explain this to Sabion and Brynn? She could not tell them the truth about what had just happened over the phone. This would expose everything she had worked so hard to conceal, everything she had done over twenty-three years of her life. This would not do, and she had to fix it and fix it fast.

Jacklyn had lost her cool and her composure as well as her senses just now and she almost exposed everything with her lunatic ranting and her reaction to the person on the other end of the phone call. What was she to tell them? What could she do now to cover herself and the truth to explain why she had acted the way she just did? Jacklyn turned to Brynn and inhaled a deep breath. "Honey, I am so sorry. This is something that caught me off guard. Sabion is fine, and no, he is not going back to jail. I do need to talk to Sabion alone though. Do not worry. This does, however, involve us leaving as soon as possible but it is due to my research and work. I have told you my research is classified, but it is also the kind of research that other countries' governments would like to get their hands on and therefore can be dangerous for us. With all the stress with the trial, I think this bad news about me having to transfer immediately just made me snap a little, darling. Why not go up and have a shower while I talk to Sabion? And then I do need you to pack a bag! I will explain things to you after I settle down."

Brynn narrowed her eyes towards her mother and was about to argue with her but the look that Jacklyn gave her stopped her argument that was on her tongue. She had seen that stubborn look far too many times and knew that she would never get the answers she was looking for anyways. Brynn backed down, sighed heavily, and slowly went up the stairs. She entered the bathroom for a quick hot shower before she would pack a suitcase for God knew why. Her mother was scared. This in turn scared Brynn. It was not just the phone call. Her mother had been unreasonable since this whole Mike thing had unraveled and then the trial. There was something big her mother was not telling them. Jacklyn would talk to Sabion about it but not her. She was not a child anymore. Hell, she was nineteen years of age, for Christ's sake.

Brynn never got the explanation that she was promised. Well, not the full version anyways, and now here she was sitting in a brand-new home in another country, staring out her new bedroom window and only new the slightest reason as to why, or at least the simplest version that her mother had told her. Sabion gave up his move to Las Vegas and his growing cage fighting career to stay with Jacklyn and Brynn, only stating it was for the best and he had to keep Brynn safe and refused to go to Vegas and moved with them instead. Sabion only stated that he wanted to give up his career anyways, since it had almost landed him in jail and had put Brynn in terrible jeopardy. They had all planned to move with Sabion to Las Vegas so he could expand his fighting career, but for some reason, their mother had said that whoever they were hiding from or whoever had made the threatening phone call knew that they were all going to Vegas and this was no longer an option. What was so classified with their mother's work had them all now living in Canada? Brynn had never questioned her mother about her working for a government organization that did classified work but now it was affecting their personal lives, and this just was not acceptable. Soon, Brynn would confront her mother and not take no for an answer anymore.

Brynn had tried many times over the past week to get information out of her mother and Sabion but neither of them would break. All Sabion would tell her was, "Just give Mom some time. She will tell you." Brynn knew that this was bothering Sabion immensely but let it slide for now as the time would come. Brynn hoped sooner than later. She hated that her mother kept her in the dark about all of it. She was very mature for her age and even Sabion always said she was an old soul. Brynn sighed. The Mike tragedy was behind them and now they lived in this beautiful country and this massive new house. Life had to get better. It just had to. Some explanations from her mother would help them all begin to heal.

Just as Brynn was contemplating their new life in her room, Sabion was now finished arranging his and was sitting in his large lounge chair looking out his window towards the ocean. He was thinking of the time when his mother had her melt down the night. He had been released from prison a free man of the manslaughter charges. He knew his mother was not telling him all there was to know either, but the information that she did share with him that night made him one of the happiest men in the world for a few hours.

For many years, Sabion held a deep disgust towards himself about his unnatural feelings for his sister. He desired Brynn from the time his hormones kicked in. Brothers were not supposed to feel these feelings towards their own flesh and blood. This had tortured him for so long.

He loved his sister like a man would a lover, girlfriend, or a wife. He dallied with some women just to release his libido from time to time, but he never stayed with one. He only had one-night-stands, and each time he did, he fantasized that it was Brynn and then that was it. He held back so many times in touching Brynn the way he wanted to. This was so extremely hard, since Brynn was always so touchy, feely, and cuddly in a sisterly way. Sabion had to fight his desire every time she was close to him and that was always. They had constantly been awfully close to each other and they were best friends.

Their mother was so overly protective of Brynn with the opposite sex that Sabion stepped in not only as a brother but as Brynn's protector, best friend, and confidant as well. When his mother told him that night that Brynn had been adopted, his brain burst with such happiness and all the disgust he felt towards himself just melted away. With his newfound joy, he almost didn't hear his mother explain that people were looking for Brynn because she was an illegitimate heir to a very powerful family that did not in any way want this information about Brynn and who her true mother and father were hitting the tabloids and getting out to the public.

Jacklyn had told Sabion that the phone call had been a private detective that had demanded that she tell him all she knew about Brynn and the family she was born to or he would ruin her and her family if she didn't hand Brynn's information over. This explained why they had to move so fast, but it did not explain why Jacklyn had mentioned that her work was classified and how this involved Brynn. When he tried to get his mother to explain, she would only say that the two subjects were separate, but it was just a coincidence that they happened to have come up at the same time.

This did not sit well with Sabion. His mother was not telling him the whole truth. There was something more about the two scenarios that were linked somehow. Sabion could not go to Vegas. That was not even in the cards anymore if he had to separate from Brynn. He was telling Brynn the truth that while he was in jail, he had decided that he did not want to be involved with his fighting career anymore. Putting Brynn in danger the way he did almost killed her and landed him in jail for murder.

He was always surrounded by men that had a few screws loose. They were powerful, strong men who loved to beat up everything around them and he just could not let another 'Mike' creep into Brynn's life again. She was just too beautiful. Men could not handle her around them without them wanting to possess her. He had to protect her. He had to be there when Jacklyn decided that Brynn should finally know that she was adopted. He had to be there to see if maybe her feelings for him were even close to being the same as his feelings for her. If they were not, he would accept her decision. It would kill him, but he would still be her guardian and best friend. He loved her that much. He would not be able to bear being without Brynn. She was his life.

Chapter Seven

As Brynn watched out her bedroom window, her thoughts were distracted as she noticed Sabion quickly walking around the pool, out past the high fence towards the cedars that led to the ocean. Brynn was a little disappointed that Sabion did not ask her to go for a walk with him but figured that maybe he needed some time alone. She got up from her bed and slowly stretched. She was just about to go downstairs to see if her mom needed any help unpacking when Sabion bounded into her bedroom from the bathroom connecting their rooms together. Brynn jumped with a start, as she was extremely confused as to how Sabion had been able to get back up into his bedroom so fast from him being outside in the woods and he even changed clothes. It had only been about a minute since she turned from the window after seeing Sabion headed out the back towards the beach and suddenly he was standing in front of her. "What the hell, Sabion? Have you added super speed to your resume now? How the heck did you get up here so fast and change your clothes?" Sabion frowned at Brynn, a little confused at what she meant.

"I guess I am always adding to my ability resume, Brynn. You should see my room. I think I could win an interior design contest with what I created in there, but right now I am famished. I was wondering if you wanted to come down and raid the fridge with me and make some of our fabulous sandwiches together and see how Mom's doing with her unpacking."

Brynn was about to question Sabion and how he was able to get up to their rooms so fast but realized how hungry she was as well as her stomach protesting with a loud gurgle. She immediately changed her thoughts to the amazing sandwiches that they always seemed to create together and raced past Sabion throwing a 'race-you-to-the-kitchen comment over her shoulder.

They both made it to the kitchen at about the same time, laughing and puffing as they opened the large pantry-sized fridge. Together, they started unloading the sliced meats, lettuce, tomatoes, cucumbers, cheese, pickles, eighteen-grain bread, and condiments onto the large island. Before long, they had two gigantic sandwiches created, accompanied by a large glass of milk each. They sat happily devouring their creations when Jacklyn walked into the kitchen with a glass of wine in hand. Without a word, she reached over the island, grabbed the other half of Brynn's sandwich, and took a bite. She closed her eyes in ecstasy as she groaned and wiped some mayonnaise off the side of her mouth. "You both could always make the most mouthwatering sandwiches." Brynn pointed to all the ingredients still on the counter.

"I can make you one, Mom."

Jacklyn shook her head and flashed her hand across the front of herself. "No, thank you, honey. I would not have this figure if I ate the way you two do. My genetic makeup demands little calories, and my wine takes up most of those which leaves little left for food."

Brynn and Sabion looked at each other and rolled their eyes. They both knew their mother was drinking far too much lately due to stress and all, but it was getting out of hand. It was only just after twelve in the afternoon and the large wine glass their mother was holding was nearly empty and they both knew that this was not her first glass so far today. Sabion stood and grabbed a glass out of a cupboard, poured a glass of water with ice, and went to hand it to Jacklyn in exchange for her wine glass. Jacklyn snatched her hand back that was holding the wine glass and glared at Sabion. "Mom, I think you should have this," Sabion said as he handed the water towards his mother again. "It's just noon, Mom, and how much wine have you consumed already today?" This embarrassed and angered Jacklyn. How dared Sabion question her? Jacklyn snapped at Sabion in her own guilty defense.

"This is how I cope. This has not been easy on me having to move all this way from my beloved New York because of you both. Give me a little understanding as I adjust to all of this."

Jacklyn's comment hurt both Sabion and Brynn. Was this how their mother really felt about all of this and what had happened to them? Did Jacklyn blame them both for having to uproot their lives and move away from their home in New York? Brynn became upset and just stared openmouthed at her mother's nasty comment. Sabion on the other hand could not contain his anger towards his mother and lashed out.

"How dare you put the blame on me and Brynn, Mom? I seem to recall you were the one that panicked and made us all move here without fully telling us why. Brynn missed her graduation and was horribly assaulted and traumatized by a lunatic. I almost went to jail for manslaughter and gave up my fighting career and you have the audacity to hint that this was our fault right to our faces. You are the one that is hiding secrets, Mother. You are the one that has so much to tell us. Hiding behind a bottle is no longer acceptable. You are going to answer for your actions, Mother. It is time to tell Brynn the truth."

Brynn sat at the kitchen island in a state of utter confusion. This day had gone from unpacking her bedroom to crying to thinking about things that she had promised herself not to think of ever again to having her mom snap at them for questioning her drinking and now, this statement from Sabion to force her mother to actually tell her the truth. Brynn knew her mother was keeping secrets. She knew that there was a lot more to their story than Jacklyn was letting on, but for Sabion to confront her about it right now was just so unexpected. It sounded like Sabion knew something that she did not, and this made her want to know immediately. Maybe this would lead to some answers that her mother had deflected from her for so long.

Jacklyn did what she was most famous for and that was to place a stubborn look on her face, shut her mouth, and leave the room. Both Sabion and Brynn followed her out of the kitchen and into the dining room. Jacklyn did not stop there. She kept on going and was about to grab her car keys off the mantle by the door when Sabion quickly reached over his mom's shoulder and snapped up the keys before

Jacklyn could get a hold of them. "Are you kidding me, Mom? You would rather get into a vehicle and drive under the influence, possibly killing yourself or someone else just so you do not have to face Brynn and me with the truth! What the hell is wrong with you? If you do not tell her, Mother, I will."

Sabion was panting. He was so angry with her. Jacklyn just closed her eyes and lowered her head to her chest and inhaled deeply. Sabion had forced his hand and she was not ready but knew it was time. She looked up at them both and motioned her head towards the living room. She held out her hand in the direction of the chairs and, without saying a word, indicated that she wanted them to have a seat. Brynn was becoming concerned and a little excited. Was her mother going to clear up some of the secrets that Brynn had begged her to tell her all these years? Was she going to talk about her father? Was she going to explain why she had always been told that she was so different and so special than all the other girls? Brynn immediately took a seat with her heart pounding in her chest and stared at her mother in anxious anticipation.

Sabion sat on the arm of the chair beside Brynn. He wanted to be beside her in case she could not handle the information she was about to be told. Jacklyn was not happy about this scenario at all but knew if she did not confess this news to Brynn, then Sabion would. She had made him hold off from telling her far too long. Brynn may hold it against her even more than she already would. Brynn may even detest her and may want to leave. It was time to speak but Jacklyn would only give Brynn the information that she wanted to and not a word more, not yet!

Chapter Eight

Adopted? Tears welled up in Brynn's eyes as her mother blurted out not too gently that she had been adopted, adopted from a family that was so prestigious that she was not allowed to know who her real mother and father were. The reason for this she had been told was that it would ruin many lives and families. Jacklyn had kept her protected all these years, since bad people had been looking for her. They had wanted to expose the family that was involved, to ruin them with blackmail and scandal. Therefore, they had to flee from New York, as they had found her. This explained the strange behavior Jacklyn had presented after that phone call the night that Sabion had been released from prison. Someone had found her. Someone was going to expose them, all of this because she was adopted. All this was because of some stupid secret her real family could not have out in the world due to scandal and ruined reputations. Her real family threw away their own flesh and blood. They gave her away like garbage to save their reputations. This was a family she never wanted to know. How dare they?

Sabion sat quietly beside Brynn, just holding her hand. He could feel her vibrating with emotion. He could feel her pain as if it were his own. He was overjoyed that she finally knew the truth, but he was torn apart at seeing Brynn hurting. Suddenly, Jacklyn cleared her throat and looked directly at Sabion. "I need to tell you something too, Sabion. You are adopted as well!"

Both Brynn and Sabion just gaped at Jacklyn. What was going on? What was even real anymore? Who was this woman standing before them that they each thought was their kin? Was anything real that she told them? What else was she not telling them? Sabion jumped up from sitting on the arm of Brynn's seat and almost knocked it over with Brynn still in it. Sabion was furious. This was not how he expected this day to go at all. He was upset for Brynn, but now he had the same situation tossed at him. He stalked up to Jacklyn, stood right in front of her, and told her to explain herself. As intimidating as Sabion was in size alone, Jacklyn did not back down. She did take a step back though, as she was not going to kink her neck to explain herself as her son loomed over her.

Jacklyn sighed. "Sabion, sit down and I will explain." At first, Sabion did not do as Jacklyn asked and stood glaring down at her. Then he let out a slight growl, let his shoulders drop, and did what Jacklyn requested. He went back to sit beside Brynn on the arm of the chair and grabbed her hand again. They both sat in silence, waiting for Jacklyn to continue.

Jacklyn looked at both Brynn and Sabion and then began her explanation. "I fell in love with a man from the lab. We worked together closely, and we started a whirlwind relationship. It was a very wonderful love affair for the first few weeks but I was young and careless and I became pregnant with his child. When I told him about the pregnancy, he demanded that I get an abortion. I told him that I would not have an abortion and I wanted to keep our child. He then confessed that he was married. He said he would never leave his wife for me, that this was just a tryst for him. He told me that he would have nothing to do with this child and if I tried to tell his wife, he would ruin me and my career. I was so upset after our argument that I jumped into my car and drove off. I was not paying attention to my driving and the tears were blurring my vision. I swerved into oncoming traffic. The next thing I recalled, I woke up in the hospital. I had a severe concussion, a few broken ribs, and a broken wrist and pelvis. I miscarried and was told that I would not be unable to have any more children due to the trauma of the accident and damage to my uterus. The man I had the affair with had himself transferred to another facility and I never saw him again.

"I never fell in love again. I told myself I would never be hurt like that from any man ever again, so I threw myself into my career, but I still wanted children desperately. When I was well established in my career and in my finances, I decided to adopt. When I saw you in the orphanage, Sabion, I just fell in love. You were so tiny, so vulnerable. You were only a week old. Your parents had been killed in a car accident right after you were born, and they were taking you home from the hospital. There was no other family of yours to be found. We were destined to be family, Sabion. We already had so much in common. Us both losing our loved ones in a car accident. You, losing your parents, me losing my baby. You came home with me that very day and I promised that I would give you everything you ever wanted and needed. When you were three years old, I wanted to complete our family with a sister for you. New laws came up about single parents adopting children, so I used my connections I had made through my work and put the word out that I was willing to pay for a baby girl. That is how I ended up finding you, Brynn.

"From a mutual contact, your family contacted me. They gave you to me without taking any payment with the strictest contract that I kept you and your family secret to my grave. Your family trusted me due to my ability to keep very confidential and classified information with my job. I have been hiding you ever since. You are both my children, even though you were not born from my womb. I love both of you as my own. I just never knew how to tell the two of you all of this, so I just avoided it all these years. Therefore, I could never tell you about your families. I am sorry I never told either of you the truth sooner. I did not know how to even start. You both were so young. I did not think you would be able to understand that you, Brynn, under no circumstances, can look for your true family. It may cost you or your family your lives. I understand this is a lot of information, but this is profoundly serious. You cannot look for your real family, Brynn! Sabion, you have no family out there that I know of. The orphanage could not find anyone that was related to you and no one came forward to claim you as kin. It is just the three of us. I just wanted us to be a happy family."

Jacklyn was finished. Brynn and Sabion sat in silence for several minutes, absorbing all the information that was told to them. They were both lost in their own thoughts. Suddenly, Brynn stated to Jacklyn, "So, I was right; I'm not different from other girls at all. This was all so you could hide me away from the world so these blackmailers could not find me. You made me feel like a freak, Mom. You should have trusted me with this information sooner. I feel I would have understood. You saved me from a possibly horrible life. How could you not think that I would not love you as I always have?"

Jacklyn responded to this by snorting very unladylike. "Brynn, you are extremely different from other girls. I still cannot express enough how different you are. This will be for another time though. I just cannot tell you any more at this time." Brynn started to protest but Jacklyn raised her hand, and that stubborn look came over her face again. Brynn knew that they had dug out all the information they could from Jacklyn today. She would get no more information out of her mother right now. Besides, Jacklyn looked deflated and exhausted. Did she really want to hear any more information today anyways? There was so much to absorb about what they had both been told. Jacklyn was her adoptive mother. She had a real family scandal that she was not allowed to find out about and, Sabion, oh God, Sabion was not her real blood brother. Why did this news make her so relieved?

Jacklyn eyed both of her children quickly. They were both lost in thought and in a bit of shock. Jacklyn mentally nodded to herself. So far, they believed her. This was what was most important for now. The truth was still her own. For how long though, she did not know, but for now, the actual truth was safe. Jacklyn stood up, smoothed out her dress, and left the room with her wine glass in hand.

Brynn knew Jacklyn was going to fill her wine again and then hide in her study for the rest of the day. Right now,

Brynn did not care if her mother drank herself into a stupor. Yes, she was angry and had broken feelings for her mother and her secrets, but right now she was concerned only about Sabion. Would this put a wedge in their precious relationship? Would things change between the two of them? Brynn knew that on her side of things, Sabion was still her best friend and always would be. Would Sabion feel the same way though? Sabion was still sitting silently holding Brynn's hand. It was large, warm, and comforting. Brynn's heart went out to him. Was he upset? How was he digesting all this information?

Brynn squeezed Sabion's hand and smiled at him. "Sabe, are you okay?" Sabion looked down at Brynn and thought how beautiful she was. All the information she had just thrown at her and here she was concerned about him and asking if he was okay. He did not know how he felt about what he had heard today. He was shell-shocked for sure. He thought he was just going to hear his mom explain to Brynn about her adoption, then *bam*, out of nowhere he was hit with his own disturbing news. What a surprising day this was turning out to be! So much information and emotion were all packed into just one hour. Never in his wildest imagination would he have guessed any of this was going to happen when he woke up this morning.

This could have all been avoided if their mother had just been upfront and honest with them a long time ago. Maybe things would have been different. Maybe Brynn's attack would have never happened if they had known that Brynn had to stay sheltered. Maybe he would still be fighting and them all living happily in Las Vegas. Maybe, maybe, maybe!

Sabion sighed heavily and stood up, careful as not to knock Brynn over in the chair as he almost did earlier. Sabion blurted, "Cannot cry over spilled milk." Now they just had to concentrate on themselves and focus on getting their lives back in order. He leaned down and kissed Brynn on top of her head.

"I think I'm okay. It has not fully sunk in yet. That was a lot to hear today. I am sorry I did not tell you, Brynn. Mom made me promise. I only found out myself about your adoption the night before we left New York after Mom received that phone call. I have pleaded with her many times since I found out to tell you. Today just presented the opportunity and I took it."

Brynn smiled up at Sabion. She was not mad at him. She could never be mad at him. This was not his fault in the slightest. She would be angry with Jacklyn for a long time though. So much could have been avoided if she had just told them years ago. "Your right, Sabe. We cannot cry over spilled milk."

Brynn stood up as well. "Let us go for that walk that you never finished earlier and get some fresh air."

Sabion looked confused at Brynn. "This is the second time today that you have said something that I don't understand." Brynn raised an eyebrow at Sabion, and he continued, "Upstairs in your bedroom, you stated that I was adding super speed to my resume and that I had changed my clothes and just now you are saying that we should continue a walk that I never finished earlier. What do you mean by that, Brynn?"

Brynn shrugged her shoulders as she walked towards the door. "You came into my room so fast after I had just seen you outside, going out back to the woods for a walk. You startled me with your speed and change of clothing when you bounded into my room only a minute later, hence my speed comment. I want to go for a walk with you. Let us go get some fresh air, since you seemed to cut yours short earlier."

Sabion shook his head. "I think that Mom's disclosure today has made you a bit addled, Brynn. I never went for a walk today. I have been wearing the same clothing since I woke up. I have not been anywhere but my room, setting it up and unpacking, coming down for lunch with you, then here with you and Mom."

Brynn frowned at Sabion. Why would he lie about going out for a walk? She most definitely saw him as clear as day. She watched him for at least thirty seconds as he walked around the pool and out to the woods, headed towards the beach. She even recalled him wearing a black t-shirt and jeans when she saw him outside but when he came into her room, he was wearing a white t-shirt and jogging pants like he had been that morning. "Whatever, Sabe. Right now, that's not important. Let us go for a walk and let nature refresh us. I cannot take any more secrets today. If you do not want to tell me why you were outside, then that is your business." Brynn opened the door and walked out into the sunlight. Sabion watched her walk out but did not follow her immediately. Was his family going crazy? Maybe Brynn had fallen asleep and had a dream of him outside and then woke up thinking it had been real. They were all extremely stressed and tired since the rushed move out to this new home. Sabion just shook his head and decided to let it drop.

Chapter Nine

Sabion and Brynn walked out behind the house and headed down to the beach to walk along the ocean for a while. It was not like a tropical beach like the ones you would find in the Bahamas. It was just as beautiful though in its own unique way. The ocean was so dark. There were large, jagged rocks and driftwood everywhere with sizable pebbles instead of sand. Their new house resided on the edge of a cove, so they decided to walk to and around the bend in the cove and then head back to the house. The trees lining the back of the beach were massive and stood like guardians protecting all the large homes up above the small cliff from the mist and the wind sweeping in from the ocean. The air smelled of salt and fish, but it was subtle enough that it did not assault one's nose. The breeze mixed with the ocean spray was cool but not cool enough yet to cause one to be uncomfortable in a t-shirt and pants. As they both walked along the beach, they picked up and inspected rocks and sticks, looked in some tide pools, and watched small crabs scuttle across the rocks into their little hidey holes. The seagulls flew around darting down into the ocean, squawking or just landing on the driftwood and rocks to eye them as they walked by.

Brynn loved the scenery, the smells, and the nature noises. It was one of the most beautiful places she had ever been. It was so rustic and so natural. As they walked though, Brynn began to get an uneasy feeling in the pit of her stomach but tried to ignore it at first. The farther they walked around the cove though, the more her uneasiness grew. It felt to her that someone was watching them. They were not alone or so it seemed. Brynn stopped and surveyed the area around them but could see no one other than Sabion and a couple on the beach, farther ahead, also going for a walk. Sabion stopped and turned to see why Brynn had paused and came back to her. "I sure love it here. So peaceful and so organic compared to New York." When Brynn did not respond, he reached out and tapped Brynn on her shoulder. "Hey there, cat caught your tongue?"

Brynn was still surveying the tree line when she stated, "Do you feel that, like we're being watched?" Sabion immediately became defensive, stepped closer to Brynn, and scanned the tree line as well. He never took Brynn's concerns on a whim anymore. Too much negativity had happened to them recently and he was her protector.

While they both scanned the area, Sabion started to feel it too. There was someone watching them, or so it felt. They could not see anyone, but that sensation was there. They both felt it now. Sabion grabbed Brynn's hand and was about to say they should head back when they heard someone saying 'hello' a few feet away behind them. They both spun around, startled. They had been concentrating so hard on the tree line that they never heard the other couple on the beach approaching. The middle-aged couple walked up to them with a wave and then said the strangest thing to

Sabion. "Hello again, nice afternoon for a walk. By the way, did you find that motel we directed you to earlier today?"

Sabion looked at the couple with a confused frown on his brow. "I'm sorry but I think you have me mistaken for someone else. We just moved into the property over there at the beginning of the beach on the corner of Cedar Street."

The couple looked at each other and shook their heads. "This morning, we ran into you at the diner in town and you asked us where a cheap but decent motel would be around these parts. We told you to check into the Ocean Cove Inn. It was definitely you. With your size and look, there is no way to mistake you for someone else, especially around these parts."

Brynn stepped forward and grabbed Sabion's hand in hers as she defended Sabion to the middle-aged couple. "Hello there, I am Brynn, and this is Sabion. We just moved here, and we have been unpacking all day. We have not left each other's side for more than a few minutes. I can guarantee to you that Sabion was not in town at a diner. In fact, this is the first time we have ventured out today for this walk. Are you sure it was Sabion you saw?" The couple looked a little uncomfortably at them both.

The middle-aged couple turned to each other, frowning. They were thinking that these younglings were playing a strange game with them, so they wanted to get as far away from the two of them as fast as possible. As they began to walk away, the man stated over his shoulder with a shrug, "Well, if it wasn't you, then you have an identical twin roaming around these parts. Hope you both have a nice day, and welcome to the area." With that, they quickly took themselves away down the beach to continue their walk.

Every few seconds though, they looked back to make sure that Brynn and Sabion were not following them.

Sabion was still watching the couple as he blurted out, "Well, this day cannot get any stranger. What the hell was that all about?" Brynn shook her head and shrugged her shoulders as she looked towards Sabion in a bit of distress. What if the person she had seen in the backyard by the pool had not been Sabion? What if it was this lookalike? This would make sense as to why Sabion denied going for a walk and how fast he had shown up in her room with his morning's clothing back on. Brynn pulled at Sabion's arm as she headed back towards the direction of their house. The sooner she could get back inside behind a locked door, the better she would feel. Sabion had the same idea as well but an idea struck him, and he quickly let go of Brynn's hand. "I will be right back. Just stay here," he said and quickly ran back towards the couple. He stopped them and Brynn could see him asking them a question and then with a wave at the couple, he ran back towards her.

"Brynn, what was I wearing when you saw me outside today?"

Without hesitation, Brynn stated, "A black t-shirt and a pair of jeans. Why?"

Sabion rubbed his hand over his face and then through his hair. "This is what that couple just said as well. I asked them if they remembered what I was wearing, and they stated a black t-shirt and a pair of blue jeans." Brynn almost lost her footing as she stumbled backwards.

"We need to go back to the house, Sabe. I am officially freaked out right now and need to go home." Sabion agreed, and with a quick scan of the tree line, they both went back to their house as fast as they could without looking obvious, in case they were being watched by someone.

Both Brynn and Sabion checked to make sure all the doors and windows were locked when they returned to the house, just to be safe. If this doppelganger was snooping around the property, then he may even try to break in. If he did break in, would Brynn or Jacklyn even know it was not Sabion? Life was getting stranger by the second and this did not sit well with either of them. They had just both found out by Jacklyn that they were adopted and now there was someone that looked exactly like Sabion, wandering around their property and the nearby town. Was this a coincidence? Brynn did not think so. It was just too uncanny and too weird. She felt like they were all in the twilight zone.

When they were all done securing the house, Sabion pulled Brynn into the living room and whispered to her, "Do you think we should tell Mom about what is going on?"

Brynn's brows furrowed as she thought about this. "I don't know, Sabe. I do not want to hear any more secrets or lies today. This has all been too much for me for one day. I am still trying to heal from New York, the move, and now this bombshell that Mom placed onto the both of us. I am just so perplexed. I don't think I can take any more right now."

Sabion agreed with Brynn. He too was reeling from all the oddity of the day. "Let us sit tight on this for a few days and wait to see if anything happens. Maybe this guy will try to show up and introduce himself to us and confess that he is my long-lost twin." Sabion laughed as he said this but they both did not think it was so far off the mark, as Sabion's comment oozed with more than a tinge of probability.

Chapter Ten

The next couple of days were very tense for Sabion and Brynn. They were constantly checking the windows and watching the forest behind the house for any movement or figures standing in the shadows. They jumped at any loud sounds and would run to look out the window to see if anyone was lurking around. The first day after Jacklyn had told them that they were adopted, Sabion had pounced on and punched the mailman in the face. As the mailman came up to the door to drop off the mail in their door box, Sabion heard a noise and just assumed that his doppelganger was trying to break in and without looking, he just ripped open the door with fists flying. Jacklyn had to pay a small fortune to the mailman so he would not press charges.

Brynn slept in Sabion's bed, as she just could not bear to sleep alone. She was so uneasy, especially since her attack and now this. Sabion slept in his large easy chair beside her so she could have his bed. Right now was not the time for Sabion to be distracted. He was becoming terrified that these people would come and find Brynn and do something terrible to hurt her. He also could not get this doppelganger out of his head. Could he have an identical twin that had found him? For some reason, Sabion was thinking the two issues were connected somehow but he just could not come up with any type of explanation for his scattered thoughts. All he could do was make Brynn feel protected. This was all that mattered right now.

Jacklyn noticed that her children were on edge more so than usual. They were constantly looking out the windows and shutting the blinds, checking the doors, and whispering in the corners. They were getting on her nerves and it was not even their fault. Yes, they were smart to protect each other and watch out for danger, but they had not talked to her, since she was forced to reveal some of her secret. They had shut her out entirely. Jacklyn expected to be shut out for a while, but it still hurt her. She was human with emotions too. She knew she had also hurt her children terribly, so she took their shutout with a grain of salt, but her beautiful, lively, and vivacious children were angry, paranoid, and scared now. They were both acting like someone was about to break down the doors. Maybe they were right! They just did not realize that the people they were watching for were fictitious, that the real person they should be watching out for was far more dangerous than the lie.

Yes, Jacklyn had told them that Brynn's family had enemies and would love to get a hold of Brynn to blackmail her true family but that was a terrible lie. If Jacklyn had just said 'no' to Sabion when he begged to take them both to his championship match, none of this would have happened. She blamed herself for her weakness to please her children.

Damn Mike and his obsession with Brynn for exposing her and getting that first photo from their balcony of Brynn splashed all over the media. None of this would have happened if only that one simple photo had not been publicized and made into such a widespread media sensation. The media only became mesmerized with the murder case due to her extreme uncommon beauty. This was how Sebastian had found them and directed him to where they were. All because of one damn photo!

This was what Jacklyn had tried to avoid for all of Brynn's life. Jacklyn had never allowed to have Brynn photographed, not even for her school pictures. She had kept her out of public photos and media her whole life. Brynn's beauty was so surreal that people would start to ask questions about her. She should never have allowed her to go to school. She should have kept her hidden, but her quilt about Brynn had her break down and let her go to an all-girls private school. Jacklyn had convinced herself that nothing would go wrong if she took precautions but after so many years, she had become lazy and sloppy.

Sabion was just as breathtaking as Brynn was, but he was a strong man that could survive out in the public without anyone taking so much notice. His perfect face and physique were not as noticeable per say as Brynn's were. He blended better than she did. Brynn was a woman in a man's world. Men did not know how to accept beautiful women without trying to possess them or steal them away or worse.

Now, both her kids were in danger of being found and taken back but not for the reasons she told her children. Yes, they were in hiding by moving to another country so they would not be found, but again, not for the reasons she told them both. Jacklyn sighed heavily and poured herself another glass of wine and downed the whole glass in a few swallows as she paced back and forth in her study.

All these years of secrecy and concealment were catching up to her. She was exhausted. The truth was just too much. If she told them the whole truth, they would detest her. No matter how much she wanted children, there was no excuse for what she had done. She could have just adopted the legal way. They would call her Dr. Frankenstein. They would both look at her like she was crazy and have her committed, or worse, they would disown her and leave her all alone. If her employers found out the truth, they would take Brynn and Sabion back and do what had been intended for them in the first place. Or they would all be killed for Jacklyn's actions. If only she had not wanted children so desperately, none of this would have ever happened. The opportunity from her employment at the lab had presented itself and she took it, not once but twice.

A heap of planning, manipulating data, altering specimens, deception, and secrecy were the key to Jacklyn's success in accomplishing what she started over twenty-three years ago. Jacklyn thought she had covered all her tracks and made her deception foolproof. Now it was coming back to haunt her in the most tragic way. She may lose her children either to this madman or due to them finding out the truth. These both were unacceptable, but Jacklyn had no ideas anymore. She just did not know how to fix this massive problem. Jacklyn poured herself another glass of wine.

She did not lie to her children or that she had lost her unborn in an accident and could no longer carry her own. Nor had she lied about her brief love affair with a man at her lab, but that was the only truth that she did tell them.

The rest was as fabricated as her fake eyelashes. Keeping this secret was killing her. She had to keep it up, though, for all their safety. If her employers found out the truth, they would kill her. They would come and take Sabion and Brynn away and they would kill her. Jacklyn only stayed with her highly classified government position at the lab after getting Brynn as to keep up the illusion that nothing was amiss, and the money was too good to give up.

Someone had found out her secret, not her employers but someone that was from the lab. This man was looking for them and had found them. How he had found out about them in the first place was a mystery. All the information that he told Jacklyn on the phone was everything that she had tried to hide for the last twenty-three years. He was a major threat to exposing her and her dirty secrets. If he found them again, she would have to dispose of him. She had tried to bribe him with money that night on the phone, but he had just laughed at her and told her that the only payment he would accept was having Brynn handed over to him and this would be the only way he would not expose her. When she declined his demands and told him this would only happen over her dead body, he then coldly stated, "Be careful of what you wish for." Then he warned her that he would find them no matter where they fled to. He would find them, and he would have Brynn in the end no matter what and her employers would love to have Sabion back as well. Therefore, they had to flee to Canada.

The phone call and the man on the other end knew everything about what Jacklyn had done and how she had accomplished it. How he had escaped the facility was a mystery. Why had she not been notified that he was missing was beyond her comprehension of the matter. He had been her number-one success. She was the head of the department that dealt with all the experimental subjects. She had known him on a very personal work level. Jacklyn had basically created him, raised him, and worked on him, watched his training and his growth for twenty-three years, so she knew how extremely dangerous he was, even more so than Sabion and all his fight training. He had been designed, raised, and especially trained for her employers. Oh, how she thought she was so smart at covering her tracks to what she had done. She had gotten away with it for twenty-three years, but somehow, he had escaped, found out about everything she had accomplished, and covered up. He was now demanding to claim back what he believed had been stolen from him.

Jacklyn's inner voice screamed at her, but she stomped it down. It screamed at her to sit both Brynn and Sabion down and tell them everything and tell them soon for all their safety. Jacklyn again finished off her glass of wine and went over to the liquor cabinet, opened a fresh bottle, and poured herself another large glass. This would stomp down her inner voice for a while. She drank down all of it. Soon, she would pass out in a drunken sleep and forget for just a few more hours. Jacklyn knew that it was only time before they were found again. She made the decision to tell both Sabion and Brynn the complete truth tomorrow. She just had to, for their safety and her sanity. With that decision made, she nodded to herself, took a deep breath, and filled her glass to the brim again as she allowed a single tear to fall down her cheek.

Chapter Eleven

Brynn peeked into her mom's study and found her passed out onto the leather couch. Even though she was still upset with Jacklyn, Brynn brought in a blanket and a pillow and slipped it under Jacklyn's head and covered her up to keep her warm and a bit more comfortable. Jacklyn did not even stir. She had consumed two bottles of wine and was completely drunk. A bomb would have gone off and she would still be sleeping soundly. Brynn bent down and gave her a quick kiss on her cheek and whispered, "I love you, Mom." She may be mad at her right now, but she still loved her. She watched her mother breathing in her sleep and sighed. Brynn realized that in her own way, Jacklyn thought that she was protecting her with not telling her the truth. Eventually, her anger would subside towards her mother and maybe they could get back on track with each other. Brynn would make her promise to never lie to her again.

Jacklyn had lied to her her whole life. If what Jacklyn had told her was true, then Brynn could understand why her mother had not told her the truth when she was little, but she was almost twenty. She did know her mother was still not telling her the truth or at least the whole truth. She wished her mother had, thought she was mature enough to hear the complete true version and the full reason why she could not search for her real family. Now that she did know about her family, she did not want to meet them anyway. They were obviously snobs that cherished reputation over blood. Her true family did not deserve her in their lives anyways.

So much had happened in the last two months to her little family. A suspense movie could not come close to depicting how terrible it had been. Brynn was drained. Sabion and she had been on edge for the last two days, watching every shadow and movement in the trees leading down to the beach. Every creak and bump had them jumping and ready to defend themselves if necessary, but nothing had happened. Everything was quiet except for the poor mailman. Sabion felt terrible for the guy. He broke his nose and scared him so bad. She heard that the mailman had changed routes so he would not have to come to the house to deliver them their mail anymore.

Maybe they were on edge for no reason at all. Maybe this lookalike had only come snooping around because he too had heard that there was someone in the area that had looked like him? Maybe he had heard that someone who looked like him had just moved into this house and he was curious about Sabion and just snooped around to get a look? They were both taking this far too serious and it was freaking them out. They were so tired that they would not be able to protect themselves if someone did break in anyways.

Brynn could barely keep her eyes open. She was so tired. She walked out of the study and went to get a glass of water from the kitchen. Then she was headed straight for bed. Sabion was already settled in his room on his big lounge chair for the night. As she entered the kitchen, she felt a cool breeze. She turned and noticed that the French doors facing the pool were wide open. Brynn's heart began to pound instantly. Did her mom open the doors and then forget to close them before she passed out in the study? She knew that it had not been herself or Sabion that left the doors open, as they were very diligent checking and double-checking all of them to make sure they were shut and locked up tight the last two days.

Just as she was about to go and wake up Sabion to tell him about the open doors and search the house with her, she saw him entering the study. *He must not have been able to sleep and came down to say his goodnights to Jacklyn and then come and get me to take me up with him to sleep,* Brynn thought. As soon as he came out, she would grab him and get him to search the house with her just to be safe. Jacklyn probably left the doors open when she retrieved another bottle of wine from the wine fridge. Brynn's paranoia was getting the best of her, so she marched over to the French doors, closed them, and locked them up tight.

Instead of waiting for Sabion, Brynn walked over to the study and again silently opened the door and peeked her head inside. Sabion was bent over their mom. For a moment, it looked like Sabion was giving Jacklyn a kiss with his back facing away from the door, so he did not notice Brynn. Suddenly, Sabion grabbed Jacklyn's head between his large hands and twisted it brutally. Brynn heard her mom's neck snap. It instantly made her sick. What the hell had she just seen? Had Sabion lost his mind? She had just witnessed Sabion murder their mother.

Brynn could not hold in the horror of what she had just observed and without her realizing it, she screamed. Sabion whirled around and smiled. He stood up straight and pulled a gun from the waist of his pants. All Brynn could think of was Sabion had snapped. He had lost his mind. Where had he found a gun? Everything that had happened to them over the last few months must have been too much for him and he broke. Seeing the gun, Brynn whirled around and, with a desperate sob, ran towards the foyer. All she could think about was to get away from Sabion. He was going to kill her as well. The keys to the car were on the entrance table beside the door. She had to get to the keys and get out before Sabion caught up to her.

As she was running towards the front doors, she skidded to a stop as Sabion exited his room and was bounding down the stairs in front of her. "Brynn, are you okay? Why did you scream?" Brynn's mind froze for a split-second.

How the hell!? she thought to herself. Then her brain clicked back to reality. It was not Sabion in the study. It was not Sabion that had just broken her mom's neck. It was Sabion's doppelganger.

Brynn ran towards Sabion, sobbing. "He's here, Sabe. He is in the study. He killed Mom. He's got a gun. We have to leave NOW!" Sabion took one look at the utter fear in Brynn's eyes, and without hesitation, he grabbed Brynn with the speed of a cheetah and took off towards the front door. Behind them from the study, she could hear laughter and then a loud crack like the backfire of a car. Sabion dropped beside her and hit the floor hard. Brynn screamed, "SABION? SABION!" She dropped to her knees beside Sabion as he lay motionless on the floor and she shook him.

There was blood, so much blood coming from the side of his head and pooling onto the floor. "Oh my God, Sabion! No, no, please no." There was no response from Sabion as he lay motionless on the cold tiled floor.

The tears were large and hot as they splashed down her cheeks. Her rage built with such an intensity that it surprised her. The fear was gone. Her mania fueled her on as she rose and ran straight towards her assailant. This man just savagely broke her mother's neck and had shot and killed Sabion. She was blinded by her fury. With all her might, she flew at Sabion's mirror image as he stood in front of the study door, with her nails drawn, ready to claw his eyes out of his face, a face that belonged to Sabion.

With a quick, easy flip, he had her turned around, holding her firmly with her back pressed against his chest. Her arms were twisted in front of her torso in a tight grip. His hold was so firm that she could not break free. He was so strong no matter how hard she struggled. The doppelganger adjusted his grip to let go of her with one arm and wrap it around her neck as he still held her arms in check with his other arm. *Oh God!* Brynn thought as his arm tightened around her neck. She was losing air fast and was unable to breathe in anymore. He was going to kill her right now as her mother lay dead in the study and her brother lay dead on the foyer floor. She did not even know why this man felt like he had to kill them all. She was going to die. As he squeezed harder, she began to get dizzy and the light was starting to tunnel before her eyes. *It is not painful thankfully*. This was the last thought that went through Brynn's mind before unconsciousness took her away.

Chapter Twelve

Pain, pounding pain, ripped through Brynn's head as she came to. Her eyelids felt heavy and her eyes hurt almost as much as her head did. In fact, she noted that she was hurting all over. Was she in hell? Was she dead? Brynn moaned as she tried to lower her hands to her pounding temples. This movement was impossible as she noted that her hands were bound up over her head with her hands cuffed to a headboard. She had a piece of duct tape over her mouth as well. She could feel cold links between her feet and realized that her ankles were cuffed too. She slowly and carefully opened her sore eyes to peek around. She was in fear of what she might see. The room was very dark though, and she was alone on a bed.

She suddenly realized that she was in a motorhome of some kind. The motorhome was moving. She could feel the sway of the vehicle, hear the tires on the pavement, and the rough hum of the motor. The doppelganger had not strangled her to death after all, but why not? Was he the blackmailer on the phone that night and he was taking her back to her real family to expose them? How did all of this connect with this man looking exactly like Sabion? Everything flooded back to her memory and it hit her with so much pain that she momentarily forgot to breathe. Jacklyn and Sabion were dead. The reality of this came crushing down on her.

Tears flowed unstoppably down her cheeks, soaking her face, neck, and collar of her t-shirt. Her nose began to fill and drip. She had to concentrate. She had to distract herself from her sorrow or drown in her own mucus, as she could not wipe her running nose. She had to stop crying and focus on how to get out of her bindings so she could save herself. Did she want to save herself? She almost wished she had died as well so she would not have to remember that her family was dead and feeling of the mental anguish that she was in right now. The agony of it all flooded her brain. Sabion was her protector and he was gone. He was no longer there to keep her safe, to make her laugh, to listen to her, to comfort her, and to hold her.

Jacklyn was dead as well. She had been hard on Brynn but now Brynn knew why. Jacklyn had raised her, kept her safe, and loved her, even with all the secrets and the lies. Fresh tears sprang from her eyes and she gave in to them for a few minutes. Her body convulsed as she sobbed. She started to choke on her gag and convinced herself to snap out of it. She could grieve later. Right now, she had to save herself.

Brynn tried to test the strength of the headboard by pulling downwards on her arms against the cuffs. She was in a motorhome and they were cardboard boxes on wheels for the strength of them. To no avail though, as hard as she tried, it was impossible. The wall must have been reinforced, and the headboard was homemade but it was extremely solid. The bed was very solid as well. This

Sabion's lookalike must have customized the vehicle, especially for this very moment. Brynn was getting exhausted from her excursion and her arms and wrists were getting sore as she was beginning to rub her skin off from around her wrists where the cuffs rubbed. She figured that she would have to save her strength and try to escape when and if he decided to unbind her. "Oh God! This meant that she would have to see him again. She would have to take his abuse until she could find the opportunity to get away."

A few minutes later, Brynn could feel the vehicle slowing down and turn off the paved road. The new road they had turned onto was either a gravel or dirt road and it was very rough and full of potholes. She was bounced along a little like a ragdoll. They were out in the middle of nowhere and probably in the camouflage of a forest. Were they even still on the island? How long had she been out? Brynn knew the island was vast and had a massive amount of forest that was rarely explored. He could keep her out here forever and no one would be the wiser. Hell, no one would be looking for her anyways, as the only two people she loved and even knew she existed were now dead. Brynn squeezed her eyes shut against the raw anguish. She refused to succumb to her agonizing sadness, or she would go crazy.

After about another thirty minutes or so, the vehicle came to a stop. Brynn's heart began to pound uncontrollably as she heard the engine turn off. He did not come to the back right away though. She could hear him rummaging around and then exit the motorhome. She could feel him lowering the stabilizers and seemed to be setting stuff up outside. The windows were blacked out, so she did not even know if it was night or day. She wondered if this section of the motorhome had been somewhat soundproofed. It certainly seemed so. Brynn froze again as she heard the outer door open and footsteps coming towards the back, towards her. He was coming back to check on her. She was about to come face-to-face with her family's murderer.

His resemblance to Sabion was uncanny. It was so disturbing. When he flicked on the light, and her eyes adjusted, she almost thought that this was all a nightmare she had just woken up from and Sabion was standing there before her. The only difference she could see in him was he had a straighter nose. Sabion had his nose broken more than once and his nose was a little thicker and slightly more crooked than this doppelganger due to his fighting career. Everything else between them, though, was identical. They had the same length and color of hair, the same height, and massive, strong build. Sabion's doppelganger even had the same cleft on his chin and five o'clock shadow framing his face. The twin did not speak. He just stood there and stared at her.

When he did move towards her, Brynn shrieked behind her gag and tried to move away. He leaned towards her and looked at her wrists and tsked. He turned back to the main area of the motorhome but soon came back with some type of thin cloth and gently wrapped it under the cuffs to protect her wrists. He looked upset at himself for not thinking of this and looked down at her with a gentleness that she found controversial.

How could he look at her this way when he had just committed two murders in cold blood? Why did he even care? He was probably going to abuse her in the most horrible ways and then kill her, so why did he seem to care about some chaffing on her wrists? Maybe he was upset because the cuffs had hurt her and he had not. Brynn's stomach started to knot and churn. What was he going to do to her?

When he spoke, it was so sudden that he startled Brynn as he sounded so much like Sabion. It brought more tears to her eyes. "I am sorry that it all had to be this way, Brynn. I warned Jacklyn to just hand you over to me. Then none of this would have transpired the way it did, but she would not listen. Sabion would still be alive if she had just done what I had asked. I had nothing against my brother." Brynn choked on a gasp. So, this man was Sabion's twin.

It made sense for how identical he was to Sabion. This had been the man on the other end of the phone that night that had her mother in such a panic. It was not someone who was trying to blackmail her supposed real family and expose her. That had been another lie her mother had told her. It had been this man. Why did her mother tell them that Sabion had no known family when she clearly knew about him? There were so many questions flying through Brynn's mind that she forgot to be scared for the time being. Her eyes showed it as well.

"I am going to take off your gag. I would not even bother to scream. We are out in the middle of nowhere and no one will hear you except for me. It is just you and me. We are all alone out here." Sabion's mirror image bent down and gently pulled off the duct tape from her mouth. It hurt like hell, but she was not going to show that to him. She had wished he would have just ripped it off fast, but he did not seem to want to hurt her yet, which was a relief. After he took off the tape, he just stared at her for a few moments. "It's good to finally have you with me where you rightfully belong, Brynn."

He reached out to stroke her face, but Brynn cringed away from him by scooting back into the headboard. The doppelganger sighed and dropped his hand. "You will get used to me, Brynn. I will give you a bit of time, but just know; I am not a patient man and I will take what is justly mine when I see fit." Brynn's eyes flared open in fear and she choked a bit. He sighed again and then stood up. "This is all Jacklyn's fault. I do not regret killing her. In fact, I would do it again in a heartbeat, only this time I would do it slowly. It was more than she deserved. She died too quickly. I could have made her suffer but I just did not have enough time." At this, he went out of the room. He had to duck through as not to hit his head. He also had to turn slightly to fit through the small opening, as going straight through the door would not accommodate his massive size. Brynn was terrified. He talked about killing like he was just tying his shoe. What was he planning with her? Was he going to torture and kill her slowly like he had wanted to with Jacklyn? Why was he doing this to her? She did not even know him.

'Rightfully his,' he spoke as if he owned her. Like she was his possession and she belonged to him. What the hell was wrong with men? Why did men act like this around her, wanting to own her, to dominate her? She was a person, for Christ's sake, not just an object or a belonging. First, it was Mike and now the doppelganger. The only man that had treated her with respect, like a normal woman with dignity, had been Sabion. She missed him so much. She sobbed and felt the tears falling again. She just could not stop them.

Sabion was gone. She would never see him again. Her heart shattered into a million pieces thinking about him. He had been her everything. He had been her world. Again, she let the tears fall freely. What was she going to do without him? Sabion was as necessary to her as the air she breathed.

After she had sobbed to the point of exhaustion, she slept for a while. When she awoke again, she was still alone in the little dark back bedroom, so she began to think on the few things that Sabion's evil twin had said. He had talked as if he had known Jacklyn very personally. His hatred for her was evident, especially how she had witnessed him break her mother's neck with such ease and with absolutely no remorse. What could Jacklyn have done to him to make him want to kill her and be happy about it and want to do it again? Brynn was dealing with a psychopath.

Did Jacklyn steal Sabion when he was a baby and split up identical twins? Jacklyn must have done something terrible to have this man feel that she deserved being murdered. Why did he insist that Brynn was rightfully back where she belonged? Where did she fit into this picture? How did this man think she was connected to him in the first place? Brynn was thinking again that her mother had lied to her about everything. Her life had been one big lie. Was the story about her adoption even true? Brynn's head was pounding from all the emotions and thoughts. She just could not grasp how this was all linked together. When the twin came back, she would have many questions for him if he gave her the chance to ask any. Maybe she could get some answers, but how was she to believe the man that had murdered her family?

Chapter Thirteen

His massive frame filled the doorway suddenly and Brynn marveled at how such a big man could be so silent. She had not heard him come in while being lost in her thoughts. Without saying anything, he walked over to the headboard and unlatched the handcuffs from her wrists and then from her ankles. He motioned for her to stand up and she did so reluctantly. She knew if she did not heed his request, he could easily force her to do his bidding, so she did as he suggested. She did not want to be manhandled or give him any reason to try. He led her to the tiny bathroom and motioned her to enter it. When she stepped in, he then quietly shut the door behind her.

Brynn did not realize that she had to relieve herself so badly until the small toilet was before her. She thankfully used the facilities. At least he was not going to make her suffer from a ruptured bladder. She noted that there was a brand-new toothbrush and lady things placed on the small counter with a clean towel and some fresh clothing. Did she dare take a quick shower? It seemed that he wanted her to. Was he setting her up to shower just so he could ravage her? Did he not want to rape an unhygienic woman? Brynn mentally slapped herself to get that image out of her mind.

Okay, she would shower. If he really wanted, he could force her to have one. She rather preferred to shower alone and not have someone like him do it for her.

He left her in peace. So after her shower, she discarded her dirty clothing into the small hamper beside the sink and utilized the clothing and products that he had left for her. She did feel better being clean and in fresh clothing. She could not stay in the bathroom much longer or he would come in and get her out. She opened the door and slowly stepped out. While she had been in the shower, he had made them a meal. It was only tomato soup and grilled cheese sandwiches, but the scent of cooking food had her stomach growling and her mouth began to salivate.. She could not remember when the last time she had eaten but her stomach was telling her that it had been quite a while.

He motioned for her to come and sit at the table. The motorhome was quite roomy, but he made the space he occupied look tiny. He took up the whole side of the table that he sat behind. Brynn slowly walked to the table and sat down. She reached for the bottle of water that had been placed before her. She was so thirsty; she drank down the entire bottle. All that crying must have dehydrated her. He smiled at her, got up and grabbed another bottle of water, placed it before her, and then quietly they both began to eat. When they were done, he got up, tidied up the mess, and washed the dishes as she closely watched him. What was he up to? He was being so normal. He did not ask her to help, so she did not offer. Brynn was still frightened but he was putting her at ease a bit by doing menial tasks and not expecting anything from her yet.

When he was finished, he grabbed two beers out of the fridge and pointed her in the direction of the door. Brynn got up and he led her outside. He obviously knew that she did not have a hope in hell of escaping out in the middle of nowhere. He never put her back into the cuffs. Maybe he believed he was that good. Maybe with his size, strength, and speed, he knew she had no chance in hell at escaping. She had been correct about the forest. They were in the very heart of it. Trees were all around them and not a light could be seen in the darkness of the evening. He had a fire lit and offered her a lounge chair to sit in opposite him. He then cracked open both beers and offered one to her and took a long swig from his. He sat staring at her over the fire for a while and then he broke the silence.

"My name is Sebastian. Sabion was my identical twin. I was the firstborn of the two of us by about ten minutes or so I found out." Brynn blinked at this information and forced tears back as she heard Sabion's name mentioned. "I am sorry that I had to shoot him. I would have liked to have gotten to know him. I know after observing you two together that he would have never let you go without a fight. He would have died before he would have let me take you away from him. So, you see, I had to kill him. Now you are here with me as you were meant to be." Brynn cringed at how casually he had talked about killing Sabion. He was talking to her about murder as if he were talking about the weather. Brynn did not even know how to respond to him about this information he had just shared. What did he mean by it? Brynn shifted a little in her chair and took a large swallow of her beer and just kept staring into the fire.

They sat there in silence for a bit again, all the while he watched her. Brynn tore her gaze from the fire and decided to speak. She spoke quietly, even though she was raging inside, "You murdered the only thing that mattered to me in my life. I can never forgive you for that." Suddenly, the tears flooded down her cheeks and instantly Sebastian was there, kneeling in front of her in a flash. He reached up and wiped a tear away from her cheek before she could flinch away.

"We will rectify that as soon as you get used to me and you know the truth. They are both gone now, and it is just you and me, together. It had to be this way, Brynn. You will understand."

Brynn stared at him hard for a minute as he stared back, not looking away, but then she broke eye contact first as she sobbed out, "What you did will never be rectified no matter what you say to me, no matter what you tell me, and no matter what you do to me. I am not your property and I will never accept you. You killed my Sabion. You murdered my world."

Sebastian growled as he stood up and moved away from Brynn. She smelled so good and she was even more beautiful and perfect in person than her photos could ever be. Damn Jacklyn and damn Sabion! He would make her love him. She would accept him. This was how it was supposed to be. She had been created for him, for her to be his. He wanted her so much that he had to move away from her before he forced himself on her. He was trying to be patient with her. He did not want to force her if he did not have to. He wanted Brynn to come to him on her own. He would be as patient as he could with her, but he wanted her so badly. He had waited for her for so long. It took him over a year to plan his escape and when he did, he immediately began looking for her. When he found out about Brynn, he became obsessed over her and worked everything out on how to get to her. He had killed many to escape the facility to come and find her.

He had never cared about anything in his life. He was just a trained killer, created to do nothing more than to take orders, to kill and not ask questions, and just do as he was told. He tortured, killed, and obtained the secrets of those he was sent to eliminate. He was the ultimate killing machine and he had been trained to have no emotion for those he had been sent to eliminate. His life was his creators. He did whatever they asked of him without question. It was all he knew. Training, fighting, and killing had been his entire life until he found out about Brynn. He became obsessed with her and obsessed about finding her. His life suddenly had meaning. She had been made for him and she had been stolen from him. He escaped from the facility and from those who dictated his life and trained him, just to find her. Now that he had her, he would never let her leave him. She was his. Brynn was now where she belonged.

Chapter Fourteen

After Sebastian had moved away from her and walked around the fire, Brynn calmed down a little. His resemblance to Sabion was just too much and she would have to be incredibly careful around him. She found herself getting slightly comfortable with him already. She was drawn to him and even felt a little safe with him but that was due to his incredible likeness to Sabion. She had to remind herself that he had killed her family. He was not Sabion. He was a cold-blooded killer and an abductor. He could still be planning on killing her at any moment. She had to get to know the truth though. Now was as good as any time to ask some questions. Maybe his answers would make sense and help her understand her life and how all this was connected. If he did kill her, at least she would not die as an ignorant girl that had been lied to all her life.

She needed to know. Brynn cleared her throat before she spoke and took another sip of beer as she worked up the courage to start the conversation that may shed light onto everything. "Sebastian, why did you kill my family?"

At hearing her quiet question, he turned slowly around and looked at Brynn over the fire. He had to look away from her again to gather his thoughts for a moment, as her beauty was very distracting. "Did you know what your mother did for her job, Brynn?"

Brynn sat forward in her chair. She was a little upset that he was not directly answering her question and instead he was asking her one of his own. Brynn sighed inwardly and tried to hide her frustration. Maybe this would lead up to some answers, so she stated, "My mother never really spoke of her job. All she would tell us was that she worked for the government in a lab that specialized in DNA research, that it was extremely sensitive and classified, so she could not discuss anything in detail with us. We never pushed the subject. Why?" Sebastian grabbed his chair and moved it close beside Brynn and sat down again. He was itching to tell her the truth about it all.

"Jacklyn did work for the government per say but not the regular government that anyone admits to, and she did do research with DNA but in a way you would never dream of. Yes, her work was classified but probably not in the way you are thinking. She worked for an organization called the Decktra Corporation. She led a project for them called 'Project Creation'. Decktra Corp is a very deep black military complex organization. The normal levels of government have no knowledge of any of these black military complex operations. I see you raising your skeptical brow at me, Brynn. Why do you think the pentagon in a press conference admitted to having 2.7 trillion dollars missing from their budget last year with no knowledge to where it went?" Brynn shrugged slightly, and Sebastian carried on with his story.

"Jacklyn was the head of a department within the Decktra Corporation that manipulated DNA to create superhumans, super soldiers if you like." Brynn shook her head and laughed at Sebastian. This sounded like he had watched a bad science-fiction movie and had stolen the plot from it and was now trying to pawn it off to her for his reason for murdering Jacklyn and Sabion. Brynn shot up from her chair angry as hell.

"If you are just going to sprout nonsense, then I don't want to hear it. I have been lied to my whole life. You owe it to me to tell me the truth."

Sebastian stood up to and walked over to Brynn, grabbed her arm gently, and sat her back in her chair. "I am going to tell you the truth if you would just open your mind and listen. I will never tell you one single lie, Brynn. I will always be honest with you as you need to be with me. We are connected to each other more than you know. I too have been lied to my whole life. It took me a long time to piece together what was real and what was not." Sebastian ran his hands through his hair and across his face the same way that Sabion would do every time he was frustrated. Brynn stomped down the pain. She had to be clear to absorb any information that Sebastian was going to tell her, and her stupid emotions just could not get in the way right now. This was much too important.

"Fine then." Brynn tilted her head towards Sebastian and beckoned with her hand for him to continue as she sat down in her chair. Sebastian put a few more logs on the fire and even stepped back into the motorhome to grab a few more beers. It was like he knew she would not run away. He knew she wanted to know everything and was willing to stay with her family's murderer just long enough to hear the truth.

When he came back out, he was carrying a six-pack of beer and placed them onto the picnic table. He took two more out and handed Brynn another one. He warned her she was going to need it when she was about to decline it. She accepted the second beer and sat staring at him to continue. This time, she would hear him out no matter how crazy the story became. Hell, she has been lied to so much with the craziest things over the years, so maybe his crazy stories were the actual truth. She had always heard that the truth was stranger than fiction. Maybe this was going to be the case. In fact, she knew that this was going to be the case.

Sebastian took another large swallow from his beer and then placed it in the cup holder in his chair. He then leaned forward and a bit sideways, so he was facing Brynn. He was so close to her that his knee was touching hers, but she did not want to distract him by moving away. Sebastian continued where he had left off. "Before Jacklyn was the lead scientist within 'Project Creation', she was a student at the University of Oxford in England. She was a brilliant student and the top of her class in her studies there. Oxford was where she developed a way to crack the DNA code. She found a way to be able to extract all the useless and corrupted DNA out of the human DNA strand and get rid of everything bad within the human body, all disease, birth defects, mental hindrances, abnormalities, poor physic, ugliness, acne, the fat gene, and the whole nine yards. She was even able to manipulate the genetics of someone to change their height, eye color, skin color, or hair color. She had learned that she could manipulate any part of the human genes that she wanted to.

"Jacklyn had the ability to create the perfect human specimen free of defects and disease with perfect health and high intelligence. She was about to save the world and make it free from disease and defects for all mankind. She was a very decent human being at that time until the 'Decktra Corporation'. They found out about her new life-altering breakthrough and they made sure they had gotten a hold of her before any of this amazing research got out to the everyday regular public domains. They wooed her and placed her on their payroll. They snapped her up immediately. They destroyed all her samples, research, and studies and left nothing behind in her lab at the university to be found by someone else and took her and her breakthrough ideas for themselves. Jacklyn caved to the money that the corporation threw at her.

"They made her a millionaire overnight. From that day forward, she worked for them and them only. With all this power and money, she gave up her morals and the more corrupted she became. She was free to do anything she wished and was never denied any kind of high-tech equipment, staffing, or specimens that she asked for. It was a scientist's dream. If she kept all this secret and strictly classified between herself and the Decktra Corporation, she was living the high life. She developed a program with Decktra, and they started creating a species of superhumans that they could raise, train, operate, and control to do all their dirty military takeovers, assassinations, and murders. All behind the scenes that the regular world would never know or find out about.

"This is where Sabion and I come into play. They used male twin embryos that they 'took' from a special cryogenics lab they also operate in case one embryo dies or did not take after all the DNA manipulation. They would raise all the fixed and altered fetuses in an artificial womb. Sabion and I were the first completely perfect identical twins they created that lived. We were perfect specimens. Jacklyn, however, had just lost her own baby in a vehicular accident and found out that she could no longer carry her own children. She did want her own children desperately, so she never told anyone at the corporation that she had lost her child in the accident and faked her pregnancy right up to the end. She even took maternity leave, for Christ's sake.

"Somehow, she made it look like Sabion had died right after our birth in the lab. She then replaced his body with a different deceased baby from outside the lab. The corporation kept remarkably close watch on all their specimens and disposed of them immediately when they died. Jacklyn had stolen a stillborn baby that had been donated to another lab for research and substituted it for Sabion. She had drugged Sabion just enough that he never made a peep as she smuggled him out of the facility. No one was the wiser. If they had suspected what she had done, they would have killed her immediately. They had spent millions upon millions of dollars to create us and here she was stealing their property.

"So now, I was Decktra's only living success, as they thought Sabion had died. None of the other babies survived either at this time, so the Decktra Corporation decided to see how good I could become with training. They focused on me for a few years. They kept trying to create more specimens, but they just kept dying. A year or so later, the Decktra Corporation decided that if they were creating superhuman assassins to do their dirty work, then the least they could do was create superhuman companions for them as well. This way, they could breed them together. They would no longer have to create them in the artificial wombs, since they were finding that they had only one success so far. All they needed was to have one female success, wait for the female to become old enough to reproduce, and then the babies could be created naturally between the two perfect humans that they had manufactured. The two adult sups would have perfect babies too, as their DNA would match both parents. This is where you come in, Brynn.

"The corporation called this the 'Adam and Eve Project'. It took a while for Jacklyn and her team to finally have success with one of the female specimens and that success was you, Brynn. You survived and you were created for me. You were created to be my companion. We would provide superhuman babies for the Decktra Corporation. I would go off and do their dirty killings and you would be at the facility under close watch with the best medical attention, giving birth to our babies. The corporation would raise and train our children as superhuman soldiers and send them out to do their bidding.

"Jacklyn had other selfish plans though. She realized that she wanted a companion for Sabion. No regular woman would do for him in her eyes, as he was a sup too. Jacklyn must have realized that you would have to be the one she took in case they could not create another living female any time soon. Sabion was already three years of age, so she knew that she had to do it right away. She faked your death as well and did the exact same thing with you as she had done when she abducted Sabion. This time though, she really had to hide you away and cover her tracks, as she could not fake a pregnancy with you. The corporation was furious that their only female success had died.

"The corporation had almost given up on Jacklyn. They almost shut the program down after a few years with no success when you supposedly died. Too much money was being wasted with only one success but Jacklyn sure knew how to play the game. It turns out that she was deliberately letting the babies die, as she was afraid that if they had too many successes, then they would not need her anymore. The corporation started putting a lot of pressure on Jacklyn though. She played them and had them offer her more money to figure out how to get the babies' survival rate to climb. During this time, though, to appease the corporation, she also developed a few special beasts of war that the corporation could experiment with and keep them placated, but this is not my story to tell.

"She acted as if nothing was amiss. She accepted the larger offer of money and then pretended to plug away at creating better ways to keep the sups alive. She had gotten away with it a second time, only this time she was even richer. There are other sups now though. She had to keep some alive to satisfy Decktra. Now there are seven males and five females, but they are still young. They vary in ages from six to thirteen and are still in training. They are far too young yet to send out into the world to do the big jobs. I am the one that gets to cover those kinds of assignments. They can't breed them together yet either, as the females are the youngest, but I wouldn't put it past them to try a breeding program as soon as the girls hit puberty."

Brynn had to stop him for a minute. She felt bile rising in her throat. She got up and paced around the fire. She was hyperventilating a little. Sebastian let her walk around to let all this information sink in. He knew he was giving her a lot to process. This was all making Brynn sick to her stomach. Brynn was thinking about the deaths of all those little babies. If what Sebastian was telling her was the truth then the woman that she had called 'mom' for the last nineteen years was technically a mass murderer, and all because of greed. How many more sick and twisted secret experiments by the Decktra Corporation were going on behind closed doors in order for them to rule the world. All of this was due to her mother's research and her ability to crack the DNA code. It had all started with her mother. Brynn had to swallow hard. It was so unbelievable. She paced a while more. When she was under control and her stomach began to settle due to her emotions, she sat back down and beckoned Sebastian to continue.

"Jacklyn is not the woman that you thought she was, Brynn." Brynn snorted at that response. Sebastian continued, "She has murdered hundreds of babies in the name of science. She has played an extremely dangerous game with an even more dangerous corporation. She has played all of us, all in the name of money, power, control, and the lifestyle that she had become accustomed to. Jacklyn had become as narcissistic as the men running the Decktra Corporation.

"I have been raised in the Decktra facility where I have been beaten, abused, tortured, brainwashed, and forced to do the most ungodly things to others, all for the corporation's financial gain and world dominance. I have been given no freedoms and have never had a day off. I was constantly in brutal training if I was not out obtaining secrets and killing someone.

"The corporation always marveled at my ability to retrieve so many secrets from my targets. They could never understand how I was able to extract the information that I did from my subjects I was sent to kill. Secrets that no one else had been able to obtain. These subjects that I was sent to extract secrets from, would die before revealing any of their confidences. The Corporation always tried to figure out how I did not have to torture any one of my subjects before I knew everything I needed to know. They finally gave up and just assumed that I was just that good to their conceit because they had trained me. I was coming away with all the classified information the Corporation sent me in to get within minutes. They did not care how they just cared about the what they were receiving in the end of it all.

"You see, Brynn, I have a secret of my own. Something no one suspected or even dreamed could happen when Jacklyn began playing around with manipulating the human species. This is my secret that no one knows of yet. I keep it safe within me. This secret of mine is how I was able to find out all this information about Jacklyn and what she had done with 'Project Creation,' and 'Project Adam and Eve,' and with the Decktra Corporation. My secret is how I found out about you and Sabion, where you lived, and where you moved to. Jacklyn thought this was because of a stupid photo that had been taken of you and I found you because of the news after you had been attacked. I had found out about you a year before you had been assaulted by that maniac, and all of it was from Jacklyn herself, without her even having to say one word to me. I give props to Sabion for killing Mike because if he had not killed him, then I certainly would have."

Chapter Fifteen

Brynn was speechless. She believed that every word Sebastian had just told her was the utter and complete truth. Sebastian had been right about the beer. She was glad she had been given the second bottle, as it was already gone as she had drained it through his storytelling. Brynn stood up and went over to the case of beer and grabbed another one. Without thinking, she handed the beer to Sebastian just as she would have with Sabion and he opened it for her and handed it back. She realized what she had done, and it pained her.

Sebastian was so like Sabion that she momentarily forgot who he really was again. Disgusted with herself, she sat back down and gulped a few swallows of her freshly opened beer. What she had just heard made her sick to her stomach, knowing what her mother had done to Sebastian, Sabion, herself, and then all those babies, all this for money, power, and a comfortable life. She stopped her thoughts right there as she realized that now she knew the truth about Jacklyn. She accepted her death as a kind of justified Karma. Deep down inside, she always knew there was something off about her mother and now she understood why she had felt this way. Because of Jacklyn's greed and secrets, Sabion was dead. Tears again flooded her eyes, but she sniffled them back because she did not want Sebastian to see her tears, as this seemed to make her feel weak in front of him and she did not want his concern, for God's sake.

Sebastian held up his hands suddenly and looked sadly at Brynn. "I am happy to know you have accepted Jacklyn's death. I am sorry about Sabion. I can see now how much you loved him."

Brynn glared at Sebastian. "You have no right to say Sabion's name and you definitely have no right to talk about him to me. You will never understand what you took from me when Sabion died. He is my memory. Never ever say his name again." Brynn was on the edge; she was upset at what she had just heard and now he was acting all concerned for her. How dared he? Brynn frowned suddenly. "How did you know I have accepted Jacklyn's death? I just thought about it. I never said it out loud. Can you read minds or something?"

Sebastian raised an amused eyebrow towards her question. Maybe his ability was not so special after all. Brynn was sensitive as well; he could feel it. She had no idea though, and it was in no way as honed as his, but he would teach her. They had the rest of their lives together for him to do so. Sebastian took another beer from the case and turned back to Brynn as he opened it and then threw another log on the fire. "It is funny you should mention mindreading, Brynn, because that is my secret." Brynn almost fell off the edge of her chair. She had found out the truth of her mother, the creation and development of superhuman beings, top-secret covert corporation projects, and now mindreading. What the hell was Sebastian going to toss out at her next? Brynn snorted very rudely before she gained her composure and sat farther back on her chair and took another large swig of her beer. She was totally in a nightmare. All that was left now was for aliens to land next to them and all would be covered. Yet, deep down inside her, she believed him.

Sabion and she had always been able to communicate without even saying any words to each other when they were in the same room together. She never actually heard his words in her head. She just knew what he was going to say and vice versa. She could always tell her mother was lying to her but just could not figure out everything. She was sensitive to people's emotions and Sabion always seemed to know what his opponent was going to do before they did it and that was what made him such a good fighter, but she could not actually read minds. She was just sensitive to the energy around her.

Brynn looked at Sebastian as he sat there eyeing her. "So you can read minds. Tell me what I am thinking right this minute."

Sebastian shook his head. "It is not that simple, Brynn. I can only extract the deepest secrets inside of someone's mind when people are under extreme stress, sexually turned on, or trying to hide a secret. There must be a strong emotion linked for my ability to get that information from their heads. For example, when you saw your mother killed, you were relieved in a small way that she was dead, even though the horror of seeing me break her neck disturbed you. When you saw Sabion shot and on the floor with blood coming out of his head, you were instantly sorry that you never told him that you were in love with him, not as a sister but as a woman."

Brynn again shot up out of her chair, mad as hell. "How dare you? How dare you be in my head?" She was angry, even though she had given him the invitation to prove himself to her. Sebastian could read minds. This unnerved Brynn. She was unable to contain all this information suddenly. All her pain flooded to the surface and she collapsed with it into a heap on the ground beside the fire, sobbing. Sebastian came over to Brynn and scooped her up into his arms. She did not even fight him. She was so depleted emotionally. At this moment, she just did not care about anything but her sorrow and how much she missed Sabion.

Sebastian sighed and held Brynn close to him and gently carried her like a child up into the motorhome and into the back bedroom. He placed Brynn under the blankets after he took off her shoes and then leaned over her and whispered in her ear, "I feel I owe it to you to tell this one thing because I took it from you. Sabion felt the exact same way towards you as you did to him, Brynn. He loved you as a woman, not a sister." With that, he stood up and moved to the other side of the bed. He kept himself on top of the covers as he lay beside her, just stroking her hair as she sobbed herself to sleep.

Why had he told her that, he did not know. He hated reading Brynn and finding out that she loved Sabion not as a brother but as a lover whom she fantasized that he would become to her. He hated Sabion for that. Sabion was supposed to be her brother. The last time he had read Jacklyn's thoughts, she still had it in her head that Brynn and Sabion were still under the belief that they were siblings, and she didn't know how or when she was able to tell them the truth. He had hoped that she had not told them yet before he found them. He had hoped wrong.

He should have known no one would be able to resist Brynn. She was created to be the perfect female in body and face. Even Sabion who had believed he was her flesh and blood had fallen in love with her. He turned and watched Brynn sleeping and still stroked her soft, luxurious hair as she slept. She had been made for him. They were supposed to be a couple and were to be mated. He was very possessive over her the minute he found out about her. Then he saw her face in Jacklyn's mind and this gave him even more of a reason to escape the Decktra Corporation and find her and keep her as his.

Somehow, he would have to make her love him. If it took him years, he was willing. He was lucky that he looked exactly like Sabion. He knew she was already drawn to him because of it. He wanted her to love him though, and not just because he looked like the man she loved. Again, he thought how much he enjoyed killing Jacklyn. He could have stayed with Decktra forever if he had Brynn with him. Selfish and greedy Jacklyn just had to take her for Sabion. Why could it not have been him she had taken? Why did she grab Sabion? Was it because Sabion just happened to have been the closest twin to her when she had her plan in place and grabbed him and drugged him to smuggle him away? Many times, he had fantasized Jacklyn had taken him instead. His life would have been so different. But maybe he would be the one dead now and Sabion alive if the tables had been turned.

Sebastian knew he was far from normal with how he had been raised in the corporation. He was a killer. Would gentle Brynn be able to accept him knowing he was a professional assassin and had killed so many men that he had stopped counting? Everything would be fine. He had called the Decktra Corporation after he had killed Jacklyn and Sabion and had Brynn secured in the motorhome. They immediately put him in touch with the council and placed him on speaker phone. He explained why he had escaped. Sebastian confessed what he had done and why. Sebastian told them everything.

The Decktra Corporation was willing to forgive him for killing so many guards when he told them he had found Brynn and he had killed Jacklyn for her deceit and was willing to come back and work for them exactly as he had before as long as they promised him that Brynn was his and he was the only one that could have her. The Decktra Corporation was ecstatic. Sebastian had gotten rid of a thorn in their side that had stolen their property and had deceived them. They did not have to pay Jacklyn's ten-million-a-year fee anymore and they still had all her data, specimens, and materials that she had developed. Jacklyn being terminated was a relief to them.

They were disappointed to hear that he had also found Sabion, but he had been killed. Most importantly though, they were gaining back a fully developed grown sup female that could start bearing children immediately for them. They did not need to keep trying to grow sups in the artificial wombs that had failed so often anymore. The Decktra Corporation was salivating at the bit to have Sebastian come back with Brynn. They now had a fully developed female, and they were super-thrilled. Sebastian promised that if they gave him what he wanted, he would never leave the corporation again, as he would not have to, since he had found what he had been searching for.

The Decktra Corporation was willing to give Sebastian anything he asked for at that point if he came back with the female. All he demanded from them was he wanted to be alone with the female for a few days before he came back to have her get used to him, that he was not punished for his actions and Brynn be his and his alone. Without hesitation, they agreed. Sebastian was just too much of an asset to them for them not to agree. They were gaining their best assassin back and, with him, a breed able female sup as well. His demands were simple and easy for them to meet for what they were gaining in return.

Chapter Sixteen

Brynn awoke to a heavy weight across her legs and chest. She slowly looked over her shoulder in the dimly lit bedroom and she realized where the weight was coming from. Sebastian had fallen asleep and was curled up against her with his large arm and long leg thrown over the top of her. She was under the blankets and he was above them still, so she could not sneak out from under the blankets and Sebastian's weight and try to escape without him waking up.

Sebastian had hit the nail on the head when she asked him to read her mind the night before. She never should have let him tell her what he saw. It disturbed her to the core that he was so bang on with what he could see in her head. Yes, she had fallen in love with Sabion but did not even know this of herself until the moment she had lost him. She closed her eyes for a moment and pretended that it was Sabion lying beside her and holding her instead of Sebastian. She smiled for just a brief second and then let the make-believe fade away.

Sebastian was not asleep. He was awake the second that Brynn had awoken. He lay there waiting for her reaction as she realized that it was him cuddling her. He loved the moment of peace she felt as she fantasized that it was Sabion that was lying beside her, but her thoughts also bothered him and made him jealous, which was a new feeling for him. It should be him and would be him that she fantasized about in the future. He would break himself into her thoughts. He would become everything to her as Sabion had been.

It would take time, but she would love him. Something else awoke in him, and before he reacted to it as he would have liked, he had to leave the bed right now. Brynn would never allow what he wanted to do with her, at least not yet. He groaned and removed himself from his wonderfully comfortable position beside her reluctantly. He stepped outside the motorhome to relieve himself and give Brynn the bathroom. He needed to get away from her anyways. She smelled so damn good, like freshly washed laundry. He had found himself many times smelling her hair as she slept beside him. She smelled and felt like home to him. He shook himself mentally, breathed in the morning air, stretched, and then started to clean up the bottles they had left outside the night before.

Now that Brynn knew the full truth about everything, she had to figure out a way to get away from Sebastian. How was this even possible out in the middle of nowhere? She had to come up with a plan, so she got up and snuck into the living quarters of the motorhome. She looked out the window and could see Sebastian starting another fire in the pit. She kept her brain calm, as she knew that if she were stressed, he would know what she was planning by picking it out of her mind.

She calmly and quietly opened some cupboard, grabbed a few water bottles, and placed them in a reusable shopping pack with some simple snacks, a flashlight, and a lighter that she had found in a drawer. She then hid her little escape package under the storage seat at the kitchen table. She would need these when she made her escape if she had to be out in the woods for a few days as she searched for a town or a hamlet.

When Brynn noticed Sebastian coming back inside, she quickly headed into the bathroom so she did not have to face him just yet and to calm herself down and mentally prepare her mind. She decided to just continually think about the good things about her life and Sabion. She would just keep running thoughts about him in her head so it would hide her current thoughts of escape. With this decided, she emerged from the bathroom to face her abductor.

Sebastian could feel the hum of Brynn's mind and her changed energy. When he put his feelers out into her head, he could tell she was extremely stressed, but when he did, he did not like what he saw. Every image was of Sabion, Sabion's smile, Sabion's face, Sabion's ability to make her laugh, Sabion's comforting touch, Sabion's friendship, Sabion holding her at night when she was scared, her happiness and contentment when she was with Sabion... Sabion, Sabion, Sabion. It made him quite angry and he whirled around towards Brynn as she was about to sit down on the couch by the table. "Stop it!" he growled out and came over and bent above her. He was breathing hard and his fists where curled. He was so angry, and Brynn was scared. Maybe she had placed too many images in her mind about Sabion.

One good thing though was she knew that her plan was working. Sebastian was furious. He was breathing heavily and clenching his jaw, trying to keep himself in check. Sebastian was very frightening in this state, so she needed to calm him down and distract him from possibly hitting her. A slap from him may render her unconscious. She had to keep him from finding out how she wanted to escape but not get herself hurt in the process.

She quickly decided to distract him by reaching out and lightly stroking her hand down his arm and then wound her fingers into his. "I am sorry, Sebastian. I just miss him so much. I see you and it just happens; you are so much like him." It made her a little sick to her stomach to touch the man that had killed Sabion, but she had to, to calm him down. She began to caress his hand with her thumb as she held it. It worked. He looked down at her hand in his and stared at it for a moment. She could sense his anger melting away with her touch. Sebastian turned without letting her release his hand and sat down beside her. He continued looking at their hands linked together as if in a trance. "I have waited a long time to hold your hand, Brynn. They look so right together." Brynn did not like touching him, but it was distracting him. They sat there like that for over ten minutes, with him just watching their entwined hands.

Brynn cleared her throat and tried to move away but Sebastian would not let her right away. "I'm very hungry, Sebastian. Would you mind if I made us some breakfast?" Sebastian looked at Brynn and suddenly in a heartbeat, he had twisted around, raised himself over her, and was holding her face between his hands and was kissing her. Brynn's stomach twisted into knots. *Oh God!* Had her touch pushed him too far and now he thought that she was willing to have him accost her? His lips were demanding, and he was trying to force his tongue into her mouth. His hands were roaming all over her and then they were squeezing her breasts too hard. He was hurting her. Brynn was able to tear her face away enough to gasp out, "You're hurting me."

Sebastian came to his senses with Brynn's statement and immediately pulled himself off her and ran his hands through his hair and over his face. He then bolted up and slammed out of the motorhome. Brynn's lips were throbbing, and her chest hurt like hell where he had squeezed her. She would have bruises all over her torso in the coming afternoon. Touching him was now very much not a good way to calm him down. It may have changed his thoughts from slapping her in anger but the danger of what his thoughts changed to was even more unacceptable. She had to escape tonight, or she would be in trouble. She did not think he would be able to control himself like he had the previous night beside her, so she decided she was not going to find out.

To keep her mind from giving her escape plan over to Sebastian, she had to keep herself distracted. Menial tasks were her best option right now. She just had to do this for the day, and she would be out tonight. Brynn started looking around and found some pancake batter, hash browns, and bacon, so she began to make breakfast for them both to keep her mind occupied. Meanwhile, outside, Sebastian was furious with himself. He has been close to taking Brynn without her consent. He just lost all reasonable thought as his body gave in to his desires. She felt and tasted so good.

He was usually so in control of himself with all his training. Brynn was his weakness. He was not himself around her. One half of him wanted to dominate her, own her, and to have her fulfill all his desires. He wanted to force her to love him, to control her. The other half of him wanted her to come to him, to fall in love with him on her own terms, come to him with her desires, and touch him without him forcing her because she wanted to.

When she had stroked his arm and then entwined her fingers in his, he lost himself to the sensation. The feeling of being touched was very foreign to him. No one ever touched him in a loving, caring manner before. It felt so unbelievably wonderful with her hand in his. He could not stop looking at both their hands curled up together. He was so happy just then, but then his ridiculous need for her raged its ugly head and he caved. He never intended to hurt her but his need for her was so strong that he lost all control. He knew he was going to take her tonight even if she fought him though.

He had to get this desperate need for her and her body out of his system just enough so he could concentrate. He would claim his right to her the way it was meant to be. He had wanted to spend time with her alone but decided he had the rest of his life to get to know her and the danger of her trying to escape was weighing on him. They would leave tomorrow and start on getting her back to Decktra where she could not escape him.

Brynn was almost done making breakfast when she saw Sebastian on a cellphone. Who was he calling? This eased her mind a little, as they must not be too far from civilization if he had cellphone service. This calmed her immensely. All she would have to do when she escaped was find out the right direction to go. She knew she would have to stick close to the dirt road they had come in on and then go left when she reached the pavement, as she remembered that they had turned right onto this road the night before. Brynn began setting the table to make her mind shut down so Sebastian could not read her thoughts.

Sebastian felt better after he hung up from talking to Decktra. It was all arranged. First, Sebastian had to get Brynn off the island using the island ferry service at the Swartz Bay terminal at 10:35 a.m. and the tickets would be already paid for. They would have a private plane arranged for him at hangar 6B, at the Vancouver International Airport in Richmond British Columbia with all the paperwork ready at the gate. All he had to do was drive to the entrance of the private hangars and state his name and a passcode and no questions would be asked. They would fly from Vancouver back to the John F. Kennedy International Airport in New York and they would have a limo waiting for them to take them back to the Decktra headquarters located at Staten Island.

Sebastian had one more night alone with Brynn to just enjoy her before he would let his training kick in and he became the Sebastian that was trained for stealth, secrecy, and efficiency. He put the phone in his pocket and turned to go back into the motorhome with the smell of pancakes and bacon wafting out towards him. He smiled. She had cooked them breakfast. How sweet of her! Today was the first day of the rest of his life with Brynn and for the first time in his life, he felt happy.

Chapter Seventeen

Sebastian was elated when he found out that Brynn could cook and cook well. He devoured the pancakes, bacon, and hash browns put before them. He devoured the extra leftovers as well as what was left on Brynn's plate that she did not finish. Brynn was silent the whole time, but Sebastian was grateful, as he was feeling guilty for what he had done to Brynn earlier. Tonight, though, he would take what was his and not feel guilty about it. He would make it up to her later, but he just had to get a taste of what was rightfully his. He knew that if he did not take the chance tonight, he would be very distracted for the mission of getting them both back to Decktra and possibly make a mistake.

They both did the dishes together and tidied up the motorhome in silence. Brynn was constantly thinking of her past life to keep herself from revealing her plan of escape. Sebastian kept out of Brynn's head after a while. It upset him to see how happy she had been with Sabion but was looking forward to tonight. Brynn, however, was mentally exhausted though and took herself to the bedroom for a nap. She was going to need to be awake and alert to put her plan into action and get herself out of the forest in the darkness.

Sebastian let her sleep and went back outside with a beer and sat by the fire. He rehashed the plan Decktra had come up with to get them back to the Corporation. It was simple enough. The hardest part would be keeping Brynn hidden and silent in the motorhome on the ferry ride.

He had made sure the bedroom in the motorhome was sturdy, so if she struggled, the motorhome would not sway back and forth. He had reinforced the bed and the headboard with steel. On the inside of the bedroom, Sebastian had also made the walls steel-plated with extra foam insulation as well to be a little more soundproof. The windows were blacked out, so no one would be able to peek inside and see her tied up on the bed. He would make sure she was handcuffed again as well as gagged. He would put her into a sleeping bag and tie her down to the bed so she would not be able to move or struggle too much. It would be for only an hour and a half. He did not want her to be too uncomfortable, but it had to be done so no one would become suspicious.

Brynn's nap had lasted several hours. When she woke up, it was already late afternoon. She could smell something cooking on the barbecue. She had not eaten much for breakfast due to her nerves and constant concentration of her thoughts. Now she was quite hungry. She got up and headed outside. Brynn exited the motorhome and walked over to the fire where Sebastian was turning steaks and went over to her chair and sat down. If only this had been Sabion! She fantasized about it, being out here in the beauty of the forest, camping and relaxing, and that it was Sabion cooking the steaks and them just enjoying each other as a couple.

Brynn was lost in this thought as she stared into the fire. Sebastian glared over at Brynn.

Damn her and her thoughts! Jealousy flared up hot and fast in the pit of his stomach. He stomped over to the picnic table and grabbed another beer for himself and one for Brynn. He used to enjoy the fact that he could read people's minds but now he wished he could stop filtering into Brynn's head. It was almost an obsession with him to glimpse into her brain to see what she was thinking. It was a safety measure to make sure she was not planning anything as well. He opened the beers and headed over to stand in front of her. Brynn went to take the beer that Sebastian had handed to her, but he held it firmly. They stared at each other, both holding the beer when Sebastian stated, "Don't push me, Brynn. I can only take so much. It seems to me you are thinking this way on purpose. What is really in that beautiful head of yours?"

Brynn blanched. *Could he really tell that I am hiding something? Oh God! I have to be more careful.* Brynn had to calm down and think of something else to keep him away from her real reasons for her thoughts about Sabion. "I am sorry, Sebastian. I am not meaning to; you must understand my side and my stress about what happened. You killed my mother. You killed Sabion. You tell me all the strange truth about our lives and what we really are. I have been lied to my whole life by a woman I thought was my flesh and blood. I found out my brother is not my brother. I was taken against my own freewill by you and here I am just trying to keep my sanity. I keep thinking about the good things just so I can still hold it together. Please be patient with me,

Sebastian. It is all still too fresh to be able to just get over it because you want me to."

Sebastian let go of the beer and sighed. She was right. He was being far too unreasonable with Brynn and expecting her to just get over the death of her family. He had altered her life, not the other way around. He was used to all this death and mayhem. Brynn was not. He had to remember this was all new to her. She had been very sheltered of the real world by Jacklyn because of who she was. "You're right, Brynn. I am being selfish towards you and your feelings. I will learn as you will. We have our whole lives to get to know each other and I must remember this is not how you were raised as I have been. I will try but you must stop being so mentally visual about Sabion. I do not know how much longer I can control myself with you when you keep throwing him in my face with your thoughts."

Brynn frowned and stated, "Then stay out of my head, Sebastian. I did not invite you in there. My mind is my private and personal space. I have the right to think the way I choose. Stay out of my head and you will not have to see what I think or feel. This is on you, not on me." Sebastian ran his hands through his hair and then took another large swallow of his beer. He then busied himself with the care of the steaks on the grill over the fire. She was right. For a while, he would stay out of her head. Besides, where would she go if she tried to escape? He was trained to find and retrieve people with ease. She was too tiny to try and overpower him. She had nowhere to go. It was fueling his jealousy by being in her head anyways, so for tonight, he would stop. He would just enjoy her and do as he had thought in her head. He would just pretend for tonight. He would just enjoy the camping like they were a couple out on a trip. This thought made Sebastian relax. Playing the couple would be nice. It would show him how their future together would feel like and he would relish in it.

Just by the sudden relaxation in Sebastian's body language, Brynn knew she had won this round. She had made him decide to stay out of her head for a while. She would still have to keep her thoughts guarded but not so heavily that they exhausted her. She focused on getting a side salad made, since all the ingredients were sitting on the table, and set up the utensils and plates. Sebastian relaxed even more as the illusion felt nice. For the evening, they would just enjoy each other's company.

Chapter Eighteen

After they had eaten and had cleaned up after themselves, they sat for a while and watched the sun go down behind a mountain and the stars start to come out. Even with all the stress, it was a beautiful evening. Sebastian asked Brynn a little about how she was brought up and what it was she liked to do. He never mentioned Sabion, though, which relieved Brynn. She would not have answered those kinds of questions if he had tried anyways. Brynn also asked Sebastian more about his upbringing and was sorry that she did. Hearing how he was raised so coldly and violently made her shudder. She started to understand him more though. Sebastian was a deadly weapon created for the sole justification of the Decktra Corporation and their greed. She was beginning to feel sorry for him and this was not a good thing. She did not want to start falling into a 'Stockholm-syndrome' scenario with Sebastian. She could not risk bonding with her captor.

She had to remember that he had murdered Sabion and Jacklyn in cold blood, even though now she agreed that it was for the better for the world that Jacklyn was dead. None of this was her fault and Sebastian could have made other decisions about his own life without ruining hers. She was still escaping tonight no matter how sorry she felt for him. Again, she found herself relieved that Jacklyn was dead. With all the lies and the deceit that she had spewed, she had gotten what she deserved. She would have rather seen Jacklyn go to jail though than have witnessed her neck being snapped. Jacklyn deserved to rot in jail for what she had done to all of them. She should have had to face justice.

Brynn was becoming nervous as they sat watching the fire together. Sebastian had his chair close beside hers and their knees were touching. After they had cleaned up and had sat down to watch the fire, Sebastian had gently taken her hand in his. Brynn had been frightened to snatch her hand back. Letting him hold her hand and lean his knee against hers was keeping him relaxed and out of her head though. Now was the time for her to put her plan into action. She shifted in her chair and stated, "As nice as this is, Sebastian, I really have to use the washroom if that is okay. The beers are going through me like water." He reluctantly let her hand go but stated, "Don't be too long or I will come looking for you." He was smiling at her when he said that though, so to relieve his anxiety, and just to be safe, she smiled back at him and squeezed his hand before she let it go.

She made sure that she did not hurry into the motorhome in case it would make him suspicious. She entered the motorhome as calmly as she could. She then entered the bathroom as she did have to use it. She had not lied about that. It may be the last time she was able to use a toilet for a day or so and did not want to have to stop and pee for the first few hours after her escape and waste time. When she came out of the bathroom, she quickly removed her package from under the seat and then grabbed the large crowbar that had been carelessly left where she had stashed her escape bag. She had been delighted when she had seen it tucked under a blanket when she was getting the water and snacks into the storage compartment under the seat. Brynn sat her bag by the door and tucked the crowbar into the back of her pants so that if Sebastian turned around, he would not see her holding it. She made sure that he heard her come out, and to distract him even more, she asked, "Would you like another beer, Sebastian?" He turned a little and smiled at her as he nodded his head and turned back towards the fire. She took the crowbar from out behind her and when she was close enough to Sebastian, she swung it with all her might towards his head. All her tennis practicing had paid off. With a heavy thud, the crowbar hit its mark and Sebastian fell into a heap onto the ground in front of the fire. He barely missed falling into it.

She did not want to kill him. She just wanted to knock him out long enough for her to get away. She was not a murderer after all. Brynn threw the crowbar down and immediately ran back to the motorhome and retrieved her bag. She fled around the back of the motorhome and down the road. Her heart was pounding as she ran with as much speed as her legs would allow. She had to get as much distance from Sebastian as she could before he came to. To her surprise and fear, she heard her name screamed out only a few seconds into her run. "Oh, shit!" Brynn mumbled to herself. She had not hit him hard enough and now he was coming after her. She tripped in a pothole like the stupid women did in the movies as she turned when she heard her name screamed out. As she frantically picked herself up from the road, she could hear him coming up fast. His running was hard, and he was gaining on her quickly.

She turned off the road and into the trees. Just maybe she would be able to lose him in the forest. As she ran, the trees scratched and ripped at her clothing and her bare skin. She was so scared that she did not notice and just kept tearing through the trees. She even lost her bag in the process but did not dare stop to try and retrieve it. She could hear him smashing in the trees behind her and he was gaining on her still. Brynn panicked and tried to change direction. The bad thing was that she chose the wrong direction and came upon a cliff. She would have run right off it had it not been for a full moon. She screeched to a halt and tried to decide where to go when Sebastian was right behind her. He grabbed her roughly, turning her around, scooping her up, and flipping her over and onto his shoulder.

Brynn kicked and screamed for him to let her go. She was flopped heavily onto his shoulder and the wind was knocked out of her. Sebastian carried her as if she was just a simple gunnysack. He had them back onto the road in no time and soon he was entering the motorhome and was throwing her not too gently onto the bed. Now Brynn was terrified. He looked so angry. He grabbed the handcuffs and slammed them onto her wrists and had her attached to the headboard again. He then tore off a piece of duct tape he grabbed from the small dresser and slapped it onto her mouth. He had her feet cuffed again and when he had her secured, he just stared down at her, breathing heavily as his hair draped wet from sweat and disheveled over his face. He looked like a mad mountain man.

Sebastian turned away from Brynn and paced back and forth and up and down the motorhome a few times to calm down. He could not believe he had let his guard down so much so that she was able to attack him. She was damn smart. Now he knew why she had kept her thoughts so full of Sabion. It was to distract him from her true thoughts, and it had worked. He placed his hand to the back of his head and felt a large welt. When he looked at his hand, it had blood on it. If she had been any stronger, she would have succeeded in knocking him out. "Damn it!" She had almost gotten away from him. He was upset with himself where she was concerned. Brynn had almost bested him without any training. This surprised and pleased him. Never again though. He would make sure that she was securely tied up for the rest of their journey until he got her back to the facility.

He came back into the bedroom and bent down to Brynn. She tried to shy away as his eyes glowed and looked a little crazy. "That was good, Brynn. You almost had me. I like this fight in you. We are a perfect match, you and me. Because of this little stunt though, I must keep you tied up from now on. We cannot have another incident like this now, can we?" He ripped off the duct tape and kissed her hard on the mouth and then replaced the tape when he was done. He double-checked all her cuffs and when he was satisfied, he left her in the dark and closed the door.

Brynn was so mad at herself. She had been so close. Why had she not hit him harder? His head must be made of titanium. Now she was tied up and had no way of escape. What the hell was she supposed to do now? She wanted to cry but her adrenaline was still pounding through her body.

She knew that they would no longer stay out here. He would have to take her somewhere so she could not escape. She would have to try and make a new plan but first she had to be patient and find out where he was going to take her before she could develop a way to save herself.

Sebastian took himself outside and gathered up the chairs and all his camping supplies and loaded them back into the motorhome. He decided that he would drive overnight to get to the Ferry and just park and wait for their loading time. He was so angry but not with Brynn; she impressed him with what she had almost accomplished. He was angry with himself for letting his guard down so much. He was trained so much better than this. All of this was a new experience for him, and he never had this reaction for anyone before. Brynn was making him careless. This would change when he got used to having her around him so much, at least he hoped. She was just so distracting. He could look at her all day and never get tired with what he saw. She was mesmerizing. He would just have to wait to get back to the Decktra facility before he could let his guard down with her again. He should have just taken her back the minute he had obtained her.

Brynn heard the motorhome start up and begin its wide turn as they headed back down the dirt road back towards the highway. Where was he taking her now? Hopefully, he was taking her back to civilization and then just maybe she would get a chance to escape again. She blew it the first time and now he was ready for anything else she would try. She may have ruined her chances for the next while. She may have to endure being with Sebastian for a long time before he became a little more trustful towards her. This thought scared her though. She knew he would not be able to resist touching her. He had a hard-enough time with this already and they had only been together for less than forty-eight hours. Staying with him for days, she knew that he would take advantage of her.

They drove for a few hours when she could feel the motorhome slowing down and turn into somewhere that they may be stopping for the night. She could not move much the way she was cuffed to the bed. There was no use trying to see out the blackened windows. She just prayed Sebastian did not come back again. She was scared that he would not leave her alone and take advantage of her tied the way she was and maybe even rape her. She got her wish though. He never came back to even check on her. She heard him exit the motorhome and never heard him come back in, and after a while, she fell asleep.

Chapter Nineteen

Brynn was shaken awake by Sebastian and as she was waking up, he uncuffed her from the headboard only but kept her handcuffs on her wrists and ankles. He never said a word and just took her to the bathroom and shut the door. He was being incredibly careful with her now, as she could hear him waiting just outside the door. A little embarrassed that he would hear her, she used the facilities and splashed some water on her face.

Without warning, he opened the door and pulled her back to the bedroom. Before he had her laid back down on the bed, he placed a sleeping bag on top of it. He unzipped it and motioned her to get inside of it. His look made her not even hesitate. Brynn lay on top of the sleeping bag and he zipped her up inside, only leaving her hands above her head so he could cuff them to the headboard. When she was secured to the headboard, he began wrapping a rope around her and under the mattress. Sebastian was not taking any chances. Brynn wondered if they were going to be in a public area with the motorhome and he had to keep her from moving.

When Sebastian was done wrapping the rope and tying it securely around her legs and hips, he double-checked her cuffs and then replaced the duct tape on her mouth with another piece over top in a crisscross shape. When this was done, Sebastian leaned over and whispered in her ear, "I am sorry I have to do this, Brynn, but you give me no choice." He went out into the kitchen space and she could hear him rummaging around. He came back in and her eyes widened. Sebastian held a syringe and he walked over to Brynn and stuck it in her arm. Almost instantly, she started to feel her eyes becoming heavy. Before she went under, he kissed her cheek. "See you in a few hours, Brynn."

With Brynn secured, Sebastian picked up the tickets from the ferry terminal and drove in line to be loaded onto the ferry. Everything went smoothly and he shut off the motor. They were boxed in, as all the other vehicles were loaded in a way that would not have too much weight from one side to the other. Sebastian went back to check on Brynn and she was in a sound drug-induced sleep. He sat on the side of the bed and stroked her cheek. He enjoyed watching her. He sat this way for over ten minutes, just watching her. He had to get out of the motorhome and away from her for a while. He was not worried about her waking up, as she would be out for several hours with the dose of the drug that he had given her. Being this close with her at his mercy was too tempting though.

Sebastian slowly unzipped the sleeping bag and pushed it back. He watched her breathing for a minute and then reached out and caressed her neck and then her collarbone. He traced his fingers down around her breast and across her stomach. This was all he allowed himself to do. He zipped her back up into the sleeping bag quickly and cursed to himself. He was so hard that it pained him to stand up. He had to remove himself from her presence or he would open the sleeping bag again and knew that if he did, he would take advantage of her unconscious body. He may be an assassin and a murderer, but he would never take Brynn like this. He did have a bit of dignity left but he left quickly before what little morals he had faded.

Sabion needed some fresh air and headed up to the deck. While on the deck, he made a quick phone call to the Decktra Corporation to inform them that they had made it on the ferry, and everything was on track. After the phone call, he sat on the outer deck and watched the ocean for a few minutes and then he decided to go get a snack in the cafeteria. When he got to the till at the end of the line and was beginning to pay, the cashier looked at him and giggled. She was blushing, so he just assumed that she was flirting with him until she spoke. "Back for more or did you just want to see me again?" Sebastian flashed her a heart-stopping smile as he handed her his money.

"You are a pretty chit for sure, but this is the first time I have been in the cafeteria."

The cashier blinked and fluttered her eyelashes at him with a coy smile. "Whatever darlin', but if you come in here a third time, I will have to give you my number, unless you would like to have it right now, of course." Sebastian frowned now and put his feelers out to the cashier's mind. As soon as his hunch was confirmed, he charged out of the cafeteria with a speed of someone possessed to get back to Brynn.

A few days before, Sebastian had made his first mistake. He had just assumed that he had killed Sabion. In his excitement at having Brynn in his possession, he never checked if Sabion was actually dead. There was so much blood. He just walked past him with Brynn in his arms. That was the first mistake. The second mistake he made was charging into the motorhome without checking his surroundings. He tore into the vehicle so fast that he did not even see the massive fist coming to meet his face with such force. It did to him what Brynn had hoped the crowbar would have done the night before. He was knocked out cold instantly.

Sabion dragged Sebastian's unconscious body further into the motorhome. He had to secure him before he came to. He could not take any chances of him waking up. He knew that Sebastian was trained somehow and would be much easier to deal with if he was secured. He dragged Sebastian back to the bedroom and opened the bedroom door. When he turned on the light, he saw Brynn cuffed to the headboard drugged and tied into a sleeping bag. His heart stopped beating for a split-second at the sight of Brynn this way, but he kept it together for both their sakes. When he got Sebastian secured, then he would tend to Brynn.

He noted the handcuffs on Brynn's wrists and dug into Sebastian's pocket for a key, and sure enough he found it in his front pocket of his jeans. He quickly dragged Sebastian onto the bed beside Brynn and removed the handcuffs from her and then placed them in the same fashion on Sebastian. Next, he untied all the rope from around Brynn's body and again mimicked what Sebastian had done to Brynn minus the sleeping bag. Sabion unzipped Brynn from the sleeping bag and gently pulled her out of it and shook his head when he saw the cuffs on her ankles as well, so he removed them and placed them on Sebastian's ankles also. Sebastian started to wake up as Sabion was putting the cuffs on his ankles, so without hesitation, Sabion punched him hard in the head again. Sebastian was out and this time with a broken nose.

Sabion moved over to Brynn and picked her up. He did not want her anywhere close to this man any longer than she had to be. He scooped her up as gentle as one would a baby and carried her over to the couch in the living area of the motorhome and just as gently placed her down on it. He quickly went back to make sure everything on Sebastian was secure and then Sabion went back into the living room and stood staring down at Brynn. He had thought he had lost her forever. When he had come to from the bullet that had grazed the side of his head, he had found Brynn missing and his mother dead on the couch in her study with her neck broken.

Panic had set in for a while as he sat beside his mother's dead body. His head throbbed brutally, and he had lost a lot of blood. He was not sure where to start or what to do. He had to find Brynn, but where was he to start? When he thought a bit, he got up and began to search his mother's study and searched through her desk. He was about to give up when he found a false bottom in one of the drawers. He removed the bottom and found a secret compartment that contained a key. He turned every picture around in the study until he found a safe behind a picture on the back wall. The key opened the safe. Inside the safe, he found many documents, lots of cash bundles, and pictures of his doppelganger that had years and dates written on them along with the name Sebastian scrolled across the back of some of the photos. There were also some letters and a diary that had been in Jacklyn's handwriting.

The letters and the diary told a whole unbelievable story. She must have written the letters over the years, trying to explain about what she had done and just could not give them to who she intended to. He knew they were meant for himself and Brynn. Everything was in the letters that she never explained to them to their faces. This was all he needed to know. When he was finished reading the letters and the diary, he stared at Jacklyn's body for a while in deep thought. Then without a moment of any more thought, he dragged her body out behind the pool and dug a shallow grave and dumped her body into the hole in the dark cover of the night.

Sabion no longer had any gentle and caring feelings for this woman that had abducted him and Brynn as babies from the corporation that she worked for and pretended to be their loving mother. Because of Jacklyn's choices, Brynn was gone and he had almost died. She mattered little to him now. Sabion covered the grave and made sure that if anyone walked by, they would have no idea that a body had been buried there. He placed a large boulder from the side of the house over top of the grave so animals could not dig up the body. He even pulled some flower plants from around the pool's garden and transplanted them over the grave, not as respect but as cover, to make it look like it was just a nice spot you passed as you walked down the path to the beach.

Sabion went back to the safe and found other documents that were from the corporation that she worked for called Decktra. The Decktra Corporation was still in New York City on Staten Island. Sebastian must have come from there to find them. Yes, he was his identical twin as the letters confirmed. Now he just had to think where his twin would have taken Brynn. He must be going back to the Decktra Corporation with her. This meant that he would have to get to the ferry to get to the airport in Vancouver to fly to New York. It was exceedingly early morning still. The earliest ferry was not until 10:30 a.m. He could easily drive there and wait to see if he spotted his twin trying to get onto the ferry, as this was the only way off the island unless he had his own plane. Sabion had to take the chance and wait at the ferry terminal.

It took two days, but as Sabion was about to have a quick nap in his car late in the second evening, a motorhome pulled into the large parking lot to wait for the morning ferry. And there he was, his twin stepping out from the motorhome. Sabion watched him as he walked around checking the tires and making sure nothing was amiss. Sabion was wide awake now. He slunk down in his car seat to be sure he was not noticed by Sebastian as he was walking around checking things out. Sabion was sure Brynn was tied up inside the motorhome. He could not attack now. He knew that if he went head to head with Sebastian right now, he would lose. If what he read was true in Jacklyn's diary about Sebastian's training, then he would be wise to wait and use a surprise attack to catch Sebastian unawares. This was Sabion's best chance at bettering Sebastian.

So, Sabion watched and waited patiently. He was dying inside knowing that Brynn was in the motorhome only half a parking lot away from him, but he just could not risk losing her again. He had to plan. He would see Brynn soon enough. As Sabion watched the motorhome from afar, he developed an idea to surprise Sebastian. The only way this would work was if Sebastian came out of the motorhome when they were on the ferry. Sabion would wait and then he would sneak in the motorhome and lie in wait for Sebastian and then detain him somehow and wait to get the motorhome off the ferry. Then he would go to somewhere quiet and the questioning would begin.

That morning, he made sure he had his ticket first thing. He kept checking and looking over his shoulder to make sure Sebastian was not exiting the motorhome and possibly seeing him. Sabion bought a walk-on ticket only. He paid for his car to be kept in the storage zone and moved it to the secured parking area right after he obtained his ticket. This way, he would not leave his car on the ferry and have the ferry security think someone had fallen overboard and start a search. He then waited out of sight with the motorhome still within his vision. He watched Sebastian go to the terminal and get his ticket and made sure that the motorhome drove onto the ferry before he boarded. When he boarded, he quickly went to the cafeteria to purchase a water and a sandwich, as he hadn't had anything to eat for over twelve hours and then quickly took himself down to the parking level where all the vehicles were still being loaded. He hid himself behind another motorhome and waited for Sebastian to exit while he ate his sandwich. He prayed that Sebastian would come out or he would be in trouble and his plan would not work.

It took twenty minutes after all the vehicles were all loaded and the ferry left the terminal, but finally Sebastian came out. He locked the door and headed up to the top deck. Sabion took his chance. The door was locked and there was a bunch of people coming and going from their vehicles up to the viewing levels or the cafeteria. Sabion had to time it so no one would see him break open the side door to the motorhome. He had to do it fast though, as Sebastian could come back at any moment. When all was clear, he took his chance. With Sabion's strength, it did not take much to force the door open. These motorhomes were not built with much strength to keep people out if they really wanted to get in. He was incredibly lucky that he had chosen the timing to break into the motorhome when he did, because no sooner did he get in and close the door, he saw Sebastian running back towards them as he took a quick glance out through the windshield. Sabion had just enough time to get in place by the door just as it was ripped opened and without any hesitation, he happily smashed his fist into Sebastian's face as hard as he could.

The ferry ride had come to an end and they were docking at the Tsawwassen ferry terminal near Vancouver. Brynn was still unconscious on the couch and Sebastian was still knocked out in the bedroom. Before they left, Sabion made sure he taped Sebastian's mouth in case he woke while Sabion was pulling out of the ferry and began yelling and someone heard it. They were unloaded with no complications and Sabion now just had to find a quiet secluded place to pull over.

While Sabion was driving, Brynn slowly woke up. When the drug fog began to fade away, she realized that she was on the couch and she was shackle-free. She looked up over the couch towards the front and could see Sebastian driving. He must have felt safe now that they were away from the ferry and with them flying down a highway, she could now be free to wander around the motorhome. Maybe he thought that whatever drug he had given her would not wear off so soon. Brynn was desperate now. She had no idea where they were going. All she could guess was they were now off Vancouver Island and nowhere on the mainland of British Columbia. Maybe they were driving up to Alaska. They were heading north, as it was late afternoon and the sun was on the east side and was lower in the sky. All she could see was trees flashing by on both sides of the motorhome.

Brynn did not want Sebastian to know that she was awake yet. She had to think. Just as she was trying to come up with a plan, the motorhome suddenly and quickly swerved off the highway and onto a gravel road. They bumped down the road for about five minutes and then came to a stop.

Before Sebastian even turned off the engine of the motorhome, Brynn sprang up and charged out the door. She was running so fast. She had no idea where she was going. She just panicked and fled out the door. She could hear Sebastian calling to her as she ran away. *Oh God! Why did he have to sound so much like Sabion?* She kept on running towards the direction of the pavement they had turned from a few minutes before. If she could just reach the highway, maybe she could flag a vehicle down. She could hear Sebastian coming after her as he called her name. Then he did something so cruel. He started saying, "Brynn, it's me, Sabion. Brynn, it's me." This brought tears to her eyes and blurred her vision as she ran. Sebastian was a sick bastard, alright. He knew Sabion was dead as much as she did. What did he think to accomplish with this? Brynn kept running harder as her legs burned beneath her. She had to make it to the highway.

Her tears were blurring her vision so much that she stumbled. She almost fell but held herself up. Sebastian was even closer now as he yelled, "Brynn! Be careful. Brynn, it is me, Sabion! I did not die. Brynn, please stop. It is me." The pleading in his voice made her slow just a bit. What if it was true? What if this was Sabion? Slowing down just a bit gave Sabion the edge as he quickly caught up to her. She screamed and tried to claw his eyes out when he spun her around. Sabion caught her arms in his hands before she could contact his face and just crushed her to him. He too was crying. Brynn snapped out of it. *Crying, Sebastian would not cry.* She looked harder at the man before her, and her eyes could not believe who it really was standing in front of her. It was Sabion. With his perfectly imperfect, widened, slightly crooked nose, she would know that nose anywhere.

"Sabion!" Brynn screamed and flew herself back into a bone-crushing hug of her own. Brynn backed up from their embrace but did not let go and just stared at him for a moment. "I thought you were dead. I saw you fall to the floor after Sebastian shot you, and there was so much blood." She began searching the side of his head and gently touched the large wound on the right side of his head just above his ear. "Oh, my stars! Sabion, are you okay? Does it hurt? How did you find me? What happened to Sebastian? Did you kill him?" Sabion was bombarded with her questions and so he just pulled her back in and re-hugged her and swung her around.

"God! I've missed you."

They walked hand-in-hand back to the motorhome. Brynn watched Sabion the whole way, completely happy that he was alive. Her soul sang with joy when she saw that broken nose, as it confirmed that this indeed was Sabion and not Sebastian. He was alive and beside her again. This time, he would never leave her ever again. They had so much to talk about. Sabion explained that Sebastian was in the bedroom of the motorhome all tied up as they walked back.

Brynn had so many questions for Sabion right now, but Sabion stopped just a few feet away from the motorhome and turned to Brynn. "Brynn, did Sebastian tell you where you were headed?"

Brynn shook her head. "No, he did not. I had escaped from him the other day. This made him mad when he caught me, so after that, he tied me up and never really spoke to me again after. He does have a phone though and he was talking with someone the other day on it. He did change plans after my escape. He had planned to stay out in the forest on the island for a while as far as I know. Guess he thought I was too much of an escape risk to stay in the forest. He was so angry with me, Sab. He is dangerous. We must be incredibly careful with him." Sabion turned quickly and entered the motorhome but soon came out with Sebastian's cellphone. The funny thing was it had face-recognition technology on his phone for security and it opened immediately for Sabion.

Sabion went to his recent phone call list and there was only one number that had been called several times. Sabion and Brynn looked at each other and then Sabion hit the redial button. He put it on speaker so they could both hear whoever answered the other end. It rang a few times and then it was answered. "Decktra Corp, how can I direct your call?"

Sabion swallowed and gave it a shot. "It's Sebastian calling."

There was a pause and the secretary said, "One moment, Sebastian. I will direct your call." Both their hearts were pounding in their chests when the line was answered.

A man's voice spoke over the other end, "Sebastian, have you boarded the plane yet? We will be ready for you when you land in New York." There was a pause from Sabion. "Sebastian, is everything okay?"

Sabion snapped out of it and replied, "The motorhome broke down and I may need some time to figure out how to get to the airport."

The man on the other end became frustrated. "I knew we should have just set up a private plane in Victoria for you. Where are you now? We can have a chopper pick you and the girl up in a few hours."

Sabion held his hand over the phone. "Shit! We are in trouble. They will come looking for us."

"Sebastian, Sebastian, are you there? What is going on?"

Sabion took his hand away from the phone. "Sir, everything is alright. I can make it to the airport. Just give me a few days."

There was an evil laugh on the other end of the line. "You know we cannot do that, Sebastian. You better not be having second thoughts about coming back to us at the corporation with the girl where you belong. We made a deal, and we promised no repercussions for all our men you killed, and you can have the girl as your little wife. You and the girl are far too important to us, Sebastian. We need you back here immediately. Give me your quadrants Sebastian. This is an order."

Sabion slammed the hang-up button on the phone. "Damn it!" He looked at Brynn. "I think we just made a huge mistake, Brynn. These phones have GPS on them. I think now they are going to come looking for us." Sabion threw the phone to the ground and stomped it into oblivion.

"We need to leave immediately and get as far away from here as possible. We are going to have to ditch this motorhome, Brynn. I still have my car at the ferry terminal. Let us head back that way. That may throw them off our scent for a bit. When we get to the car, I will need you to follow me with it and then we need to ditch the motorhome. Then we need to go somewhere that we can hunker down for a while and think up a plan."

Brynn and Sabion hurried back into the motorhome and turned it back to the direction of the ferry terminal. They both sat in silence and Sabion drove just a bit over the speed limit as not to get stopped. They made it to the terminal and Brynn hopped out of the motorhome with Sabion's car keys and vehicle-release ticket. She quickly went and retrieved his car and pulled up beside the motorhome. "Just follow me, we will ditch this at a campsite somewhere close and get as far away as possible." Brynn nodded and followed Sabion as he pulled out of the terminal parking lot. Brynn was so terrified. The Decktra Corporation was a secret unacknowledged black military complex organization that could make people disappear. They had to hide, and they had to do it fast.

Chapter Twenty

Sabion drove to the Tsawwassen RV Resort that was close to the ferry terminal and pulled in. He jumped out and went into the resort office and paid for a site. He quickly got back into the motorhome and was soon pulling into their section. Brynn pulled in close behind and jumped out of the car and entered the motorhome. Sabion hugged her quickly and looked her in the eyes. "Brynn, we are going to be okay. We are together now. I am not going to let anything happen to you again. I promise. We need to talk to Sebastian. Are you up for it?" Brynn nodded at Sabion. Being with him again made her feel safe, and they had to get some answers from Sebastian. Sabion squeezed Brynn's hand and they both headed back to the bedroom.

Sebastian was awake and was glaring at Sabion when they flicked the light on. Sebastian's eyes went right to him. If looks could kill! Thank god they could not, or else Sabion would be dead. Sebastian slowly looked over at Brynn. The look he gave her sent shivers down her spine. It was so possessive, and she immediately grabbed Sabion's arm for comfort. Sebastian followed her movement and then glared at Sabion again. Sabion was not intimidated by Sebastian in the least and walked over to him and ripped off the duct tape from his mouth. Sebastian did not even flinch. He just stretched out his jaw before saying, "So we meet after all, Brother." The menace dripping from Sebastian's words had Brynn flinching.

Sabion just laughed but vehemently answered back, "You are no brother of mine." They both glared at each other and did not say another word. Brynn broke the silence as she stepped closer to Sabion. This did not go unnoticed by Sebastian and he glowered even more.

"Look, we know that you were going back to the Decktra Corporation and you were taking me to them as well. Why?"

Sebastian looked over at Brynn. "You can't hide from Decktra, Brynn. That is where we belong."

Sabion was becoming deathly angry. He took a step towards Sebastian, but Brynn held him back. Sabion spoke instead, "You would take Brynn back to that world of murder and secrecy. They would never let you leave again. They would keep Brynn locked up just to make sure you would come back every time they sent you out to do their dirty work. You would subject Brynn to this kind of life. Pumping out children for the corporation. How dare you?" As Sabion was talking, he was becoming so fueled up with intense anger.

Sebastian just laughed at him. "If you know about the corporation, then you must know that Brynn was created for me. She was created to be mine, to bear my children, to have my cock in her every night as I have my way with her." Brynn sucked in her breath. She was not privy to this side of Sebastian. This was the evil side of him coming out.

Sebastian was seething with jealousy as he watched her beside Sabion. He said this to make Sabion mad and it worked. Sabion suddenly vaulted onto Sebastian and punched him several times. His nose was bleeding again and now he had a cut open on his cheek and above his eyebrow. Brynn's stomach began to turn, and she fled to the bathroom to empty its contents which were coming up without her being able to stop it.

Sabion quickly got off Sebastian and went over to see if Brynn was alright but before he reached Brynn, Sebastian spoke, "Why don't we see how tough you really are when these cuffs are off? Come on, Sabion. Fight me man to man and see who wins. Brynn is mine. No matter where you go, I will find you and I will take her from you."

Sabion turned a little towards Sebastian. "I'd like to see you try." Then he turned off the light to the bedroom and shut the door. As soon as Brynn was able, they were leaving, and Sebastian could just rot in here for all he cared. The bastard deserved to die for what he put Brynn through, but he was not a hardened killer like Sebastian was. If Sebastian was as good as Jacklyn had said he was in her journal, then he'd let him find a way out of his cuffs himself. Sabion did not have time for him anyways. He had to get Brynn to safety and hidden as far from Decktra as he could. This was his number-one priority right now.

When Brynn came out of the bathroom, Sabion gently pulled her out of the motorhome and placed her into the passenger side of his car and then got into the driver's seat and pulled away out of the resort and turned towards Vancouver without looking back. They could get lost in a city the size of Vancouver and this was what he planned to do for the moment. They drove in silence and Sabion had one hand on the steering wheel and held Brynn's hand with the other as the car purred down the highway.

When they entered the section of Vancouver called Richmond, they found a Super Eight Hotel and stopped for the night. They were both exhausted. Sabion paid with cash as to not use a credit or debit card to possibly be tracked with. When they entered the room, they both headed straight for the bed. Without speaking, they just crawled in and curled up tight to each other. They were both safe for now and were simply happy to be together again. They both fell asleep almost immediately.

Brynn woke up in a panic. She had a bad dream that Sebastian had found them. She sat bolt upright in bed and panicked even more when Sabion was not beside her. She calmed down though when she heard the shower. She waited for Sabion to exit the bathroom and quickly smiled at him as he came out in only a towel wrapped around his waist. He was so handsome. He was built so well. She could just sit there and watch him walk around like that all day. Brynn blushed. She remembered that she loved Sabion as a woman and not as a sister. Sebastian had told her that Sabion felt the same way as she did, but he may have been wrong. To hide her sudden rush of feelings, she jumped up and went into the bathroom to have a shower for herself.

When Brynn came out, there was breakfast waiting for them on trays by the bed. Sabion had ordered room service. Brynn was famished and, with only a towel wrapped around her, she quickly sat down on the bed and stuffed a half of a waffle into her mouth. Sabion shook his head and laughed at her but then dove into his plate as well. They inhaled their breakfast before either spoke. After they had finished stuffing their bellies, there was suddenly uncomfortable silence between them. There was that unspoken communication again. They both just sat and stared at each other.

Sabion looked at Brynn with her hair still wet and only wrapped in a towel. His desire for her hit him like a ton of bricks. Now was as good a time as any to tell her how he felt about her as they sat hiding in this hotel room. Sabion stood up and moved the trays away from the bed and sat down beside her on the bed. "Brynn, I need to tell you something and I will understand if it makes you upset, especially with everything that has happened over the last several months. I just cannot keep it to myself anymore."

Sabion sighed but kept going. He just could not lose his nerves about this right now. He was not going to lose this opportunity. "Brynn, I love you. I have loved you for as long as I can remember. Not as your brother but as I would love a woman. I was so ashamed of myself when I thought…well, that does not matter anymore. What matters is I will always protect you and cherish you for the woman you are to me. If you do not feel the same way, I will accept that, but I just needed you to hear me say that I love you in case something happens to me." It was Sabion's turn to turn a little red with embarrassment as he confessed his true feelings to Brynn.

Brynn just sat and stared at him for a moment. Suddenly, she lunged into his arms and kissed him with the passion of a thousand fires. They fell back onto the bed and just kissed each other and staring into each other's eyes and caressing each other's faces. Sabion was in heaven. He had dreamed of this for so long. Slowly, he raised himself away from her and reached out to remove her towel that was wrapped around her body. As she let the towel fall away, he gasped. She was even more beautiful than he could have ever imagined. He reached out and touched one of her breasts and stroked her nipple with his thumb. Brynn gasped as it felt like fire against her nipple. Strings of desire ran down to her loins and she quivered. He was looking at her with so much love and desire in his eyes. He grasped her whole breast within his large hand and gently stroked her again. She felt so good in his hand. He had to touch and experience all of her.

Sabion lowered her to the bed and ran his fingers down the entire length of her body. Small goose bumps rose all over Brynn, as the sensation was so magical that it made her tremble. Sabion could not get enough of her body and he touched and stroked and kissed her everywhere. The heat that was building within Brynn was so amazing. She was so astonished that he could make her body feel this way. Brynn loved Sabion so much that it brought tears to her eyes. Sabion stopped when he saw the tears wet upon her cheeks. He pulled away slightly. Had he hurt her or was she having second thoughts? Brynn gently reached out and grabbed his hands again and placed them on to her breasts as she rose her body off the bed and kissed him fervently and then whispered into his ear, "I love you too, my Sabion." This was Sabion's undoing. He pulled away from her and stood up. When he removed his towel, Brynn gasped. He was so magnificent. *How could one man be so beautiful and perfect? All that power.* Brynn gazed at that power that was standing so proud between his legs. She reached up and stroked his manhood and he groaned.

Sabion lay back down on the bed and gently covered her body with his. "Brynn, I have dreamed of this for so long that I cannot hold back right now. I want to touch you forever but right now I must have you." Brynn answered him by opening her legs under him and he swiftly guided himself inside her. His shaft was so hard and so soft at the same time. She adjusted herself to accommodate his size and she was so wet. He slid into her and with a quick thrust, he broke her virginal barrier. Brynn barely noticed the jab of pain, as the heat was building in her quickly. He fit into her so perfectly. He felt so right.

This was where she belonged. She was his. Sabion began to move inside her back and forth slowly at first. With each thrust, the pleasure was building within her core. It felt so wonderful. She held onto Sabion for dear life as he began to move faster. She matched his movements, and they flew into ecstasy together as they both climaxed at the same time. Sabion collapsed onto of her and gently kissed her. He did not pull out of her and she relished his weight on top of her. She would never complain about his weight on top of her ever again. It was just so delicious. They clang to each other and kissed for a long while. They were playing with each other's lips and tongues, getting to know the taste of each other. Soon, Brynn felt Sabion getting hard inside her again. *Oh God, it feels so good.* They made love again and it was even better than the first time. Sabion was so gentle with her. He caressed her everywhere. His touch was so soft and yet so demanding. His touch was worshipping, and he could not get enough of her. They lay in bed for most of the day just exploring each other's bodies without embarrassment. They matched perfectly. Brynn fit to his body like they were made for each other. They both did not want this day to end.

Sabion was in a dream. He confessed to loving her, terrified that she did not share his feeling, and now here they were making love to each other over and over. He did not think he would ever be quenched by her. Her body was so beautiful and so soft. He placed his face into her neck and breathed in. She still smelled of fresh laundry and she felt like home. He was making love to her and still could not believe it. If this was a dream, he never wanted to wake up. He felt himself getting hard again. Brynn had been a virgin and they had already made love several times, so he wanted to make sure she was okay. Sabion asked, "Are you getting sore?" Brynn answered with a giggle but then swiftly rolling herself on top of him, she impaled herself deliciously onto his manhood. He watched her as she moved sensually above him. She was a goddess, and he would die for her. He was hers for all time and eternity. They both climaxed together again, and she collapsed onto of him. She felt so good. He rolled her off him and placed her body next to him and snuggled her to him. "I love you, Brynn, forever and for always."

Brynn exhaled, smiled, and cuddled herself into his strong body even closer and responded, "I love you too, my Sabion." They fell asleep wrapped around each other. It was the best sleep both had ever had. They were together and they would never let each other go.

They slept in each other's arms all night and neither of them moved. In the morning, they made love again and then Sabion patted Brynn's bottom and gave her a quick kiss. He removed himself reluctantly as he stood up. "As much as I would love to stay here with you and have another amazing day within bed, we have to figure out what we are going to do. But first I need a shower." Brynn bounded out of bed and seductively walked naked towards Sabion without any embarrassment and stood on her tiptoes to give him a kiss. "Mind if I join you? I can wash your back." Even though they had just finished making love in the bed only a few minutes before, Sabion was aroused again and quickly followed Brynn into the shower. Never had a shower been so amazing for either of them. Even in the hotel, they made the shower run out of hot water. They just could not get enough of each other. It was as if they were making up for lost time.

They both had trouble even getting dressed. It took them two tries, as Sabion first tried and had Brynn tearing off his clothes before he finished dressing and they dove on the bed to have each other hard and fast. When they were finished, Brynn got up and tried to then get dressed, but this time, it was Sabion who growled and dragged her back into the bed with him. They were both insatiable for each other. This time, they took a bit more time exploring each other's bodies and kissing each other everywhere their lips could reach. As they lay together, Sabion once again said, "Okay, we have to really concentrate this time and come up with a plan of where we are going to go. Can you please stop lying there so damned beautiful and go put some clothing on? You are distracting me and we both need to think."

Brynn giggled but did as he suggested as she turned to nibble on his earlobe. "You too are gorgeous. Do not think I am not distracted with your stunning nakedness languishing before me. Goes both ways, big boy," and then she bent down and tossed his jeans at his head. Sabion grabbed the jeans and smiled at her. He had never been so happy in his life, but he knew that Sebastian had probably gotten out of the motorhome and as they languished together in this hotel, he was searching for them.

His happiness was clouded a bit with that thought. What the hell were they going to do about Sebastian? He would never stop searching for Brynn unless he died. Sebastian was obsessed. He has witnessed men's obsession over Brynn before. He had almost gone to prison for years for that one. It did not end well. He remembered when they were younger as well, Brynn had many admirers, but Jacklyn had been able to deal with them at the time. He would do it again in a heartbeat if it meant that Brynn would be safe from harm. Hell, he had killed and would again to whoever attempted to hurt his Brynn. He would protect her with his life and now that they had spoken and shown their feelings to each other, he was even more hyperaware of how much he would kill to keep her safe. When they were both dressed, Sabion suggested they go and plan in a restaurant while they ate, as the bed and her in the same room together was just too tempting. If they did not leave, then they would end up back in it and not have a plan formulated yet again.

They went to a small Italian restaurant for lunch. It was quaint and full of patrons, which was great, as no one would really pay attention to them as they talked about what they were going to do. This was an immense delusion on their part though. When they walked in and waited to be seated, everyone in the restaurant started to notice the ridiculously beautiful couple. The restaurant started buzzing with whispers and talk. This couple had to be celebrities. Sabion and Brynn noticed people were snapping pictures of them on their phones. Two people this beautiful and perfect just had to be famous somehow. Women were tripping over themselves as they passed Sabion, and men were drooling and cranking their heads around to look at Brynn. Being together in a public place had them instantly the center of everybody's attention. They both became so flustered that they immediately left the restaurant, as people were starting to try and approach them as they were snapping photos of them on their cameras. They had never really eaten out together before, except at their favorite restaurant in little Italy in New York and they had eaten there for years. Everyone must have just been used to them as they watched them grow up and eat there over the years. Other than that, they always ate at home.

Sabion and Brynn ended up eating in their car with subway takeout. With one cold cut combo and one steak and cheese sub consumed and their bellies full, they began to think of what they needed to do to stay out of the grasp of the Decktra Corporation and Sebastian. Sabion was not hurting financially from his fighting career and he told Brynn he also had obtained access to Jacklyn's bank accounts and set up transfers between his and her accounts when he was waiting for Sebastian to show up at the ferry terminal in case they weren't able to get back to their home for a while. Thankfully, Sabion had been thinking and had taken the large amount of cash that had been stashed in Jacklyn's safe and had it on him. They would not use any credit cards for quite a while in case they were being tracked somehow by Decktra with the use of their cards. They just did not know how far the Decktra's corruption could reach. They did not know how desperate they were to get a hold of them. Would Decktra and Sebastian take a few days, weeks, or months to try and find them or would they never stop looking? Would they send out a fleet of men or would it just be Sebastian coming for them?

In the end, they both decided that going farther into the province and maybe even to the next province was their best bet. The farther away they could get without buying plane tickets the better. They also decided that they would find a small remote out-of-the-way cabin to rent for a while and just hunker down and stay out of the public eye. They would no longer go into busy restaurants to be noticed together since their fiasco in the one they had went into earlier that day. Take out or room service was their best bet. When they did go out in a larger area, they would always wear hoodies or a hat to conceal their faces so they would not get caught on any security camera.

Sabion would never speed, so the police would not pull him over and look up his or her name on their computer databases, as Decktra may be looking for them on any law organization computers as well. Sabion and Brynn would make sure that their real names were not given out if anyone asked, just to be safe. This was their plan. So now they just had to start driving and get away. They would come up with a more detailed long-term plan once they made it farther into the province and had a place that they were comfortable in. With their plan in place, they purchased a map at a gas station as they filled up. Brynn was the navigator and Sabion would just drive where she directed him.

Chapter Twenty-One

They were both kind of excited to be going on a road trip together, even though the reason for it was frightening. Brynn felt so safe with Sabion though. She had been so sheltered in her life. She was never allowed to go anywhere but home, school, and exercise classes and was never left alone. She had always someone watching whether it was Jacklyn, Sabion, or her driver. If Sabion was by her side, she would be okay. She found herself on edge though when he would go into a gas station or out of her sight for a bit. She would watch the space until he reappeared and then find that she had been holding her breath until her returned to her vision. They had to stay separate as much as possible as well, as they both knew Decktra and Sebastian would be asking about a couple, so she would stay in the car as much as possible and let Sabion fill up with gas as she hunkered down in her seat to make it look like there was only one person traveling in the car whenever they stopped, just for the first while.

They exited the Vancouver outskirts and traveled east. They drove through the town of Hope and topped up the gas at a station there and then started traveling along the Coquihalla Highway to travel faster into the province. The drive was beautiful with all the mountains and trees. They encountered a few elk and even saw a black bear running across the highway and bounding over the meridians. British Columbia was such a beautiful place with so much to see. Brynn was enjoying the drive and being by Sabion's side. They chatted at times or just watched the scenery go by as they drove. They would stop at rest points to use the facilities and stretch but they never stayed in one place for more than fifteen minutes or so, as they felt they needed to keep driving. After a while of driving, they exited on Highway Five and drove towards the city of Kamloops. Here they stopped for more fuel and this time Brynn went into the convenience store and purchased some snacks and drinks.

The young male cashier was dumbfounded and stared at Brynn when she came up to the till, as he first forgot how to run the till and then fumbled and dropped the change all over the counter. Her beauty made him nervous. Before Brynn realized what he was doing, he whipped out his cellphone and snapped a picture of her. When she frowned at him, he apologized to her with the explanation, "No one will believe me otherwise." She shook her head at him but flashed him a gorgeous smile and exited the station. The poor boy could not function for a few minutes to the frustration of the other customers after she left.

Next time, she would wear her hoodie up over top of a baseball cap with her hair hiding her face. This was ridiculous how she stood out. She never stood out like this in New York. Mind you, New Yorkers were used to always seeing beautiful people and celebrities everywhere. The people of New York were remarkably self-absorbed with their busy schedules and always kept their heads down and there asses up in their own little worlds, so she guessed she could understand. When they both got back into the car, they decided to drive as far as a tiny town called Sorrento that was situated along the Shuswap Lake and grab a little motel room for the night, since it was getting late. They pulled into the Sorrento Inn just to the left of the highway and Sabion grabbed a room. They did not have to enter the building, as all the rooms had separate outer door. Sabion ordered takeout from the 'Home Restaurant' and when he came back, they ate in the room.

That night, they decided a little bit more together where they were going to try and find a place to travel to and find a place to rent. It had to be furnished, as they had nothing with them. They would drive for another day for sure and see where that landed them. That night, they were exhausted from driving. They just snuggled into each other and fell asleep within each other's arms. In the early morning, they gathered their things and headed on the road again. Brynn marveled at the beauty of this area. There were so many bodies of water and trees and farms with the backdrops of the small mountains behind them. This area of British Columbia had a little of everything to see.

As they drove up a hill on the highway towards the beautiful town of Salmon Arm, the view was breathtaking. They just had to stop for a while by a rest point to look at the view of Shuswap Lake. The sun was shining and there was a lot of activity on the water already as they watched boats pulling water skiers, jet-skiers, and houseboats. What a beautiful place! They jumped back into their vehicle and as they entered the western side of Salmon Arm, Brynn saw to her left a place called DeMill's Farmers Market and begged Sabion to turn into it. It was buzzing with activity. The store contained the most delicious fruit and it even had a petting zoo. Sabion could not see any harm but said he would only allow them half hour to stop. Brynn squealed in delight like a little girl, but she did not care.

Sabion watched with a smile on his face as Brynn fed all the goats, llamas, emus, pigs, and hens. She was so free and so happy in that moment; she glowed. Sabion ended up having an argument with a ram and they laughed so hard that they had tears in their eyes. People were starting to gather to watch the silliness between Sabion and the ram and laugh along with them but then people stopped watching the animals when they noticed the magnificent couple before them. This was their cue to leave but before they did, Brynn made sure they purchased some fresh berries and peaches before they left. When they entered the car and resumed their drive, Brynn moaned as she bit into a peach and the juice from it dripped down her chin. It was the best thing she had ever eaten in her life. "Oh my God, Sabion! You have to try one of these peaches. It is like eating the juiciest, sweetest, and delicious candy you have ever eaten. My God! I never knew fruit could taste like this. I am never buying supermarket fruit again. This is amazing." Sabion just had to try one after her explanation and took a large bite out of the peach she offered him. He almost swerved into oncoming traffic as the juice from the peach sprayed all over the dashboard and dripped all down his face and arm. She had been right though; this was the best peach he had ever eaten. They both laughed as she cleaned him up and handed him a napkin as they continued to drive.

When they drove into another small town called Sicamous, Sabion and Brynn kept seeing large signs directing them towards a dairy called D. Dutchmen Dairy. They were both in to stopping when the sign said, *'best ice cream in the world.'* They both looked at each other. They just had to stop, and they were not lied to. The ice cream was the best either of them had ever tasted. It was so creamy and fresh. They made it right there on the dairy. There was a long lineup of tourists in buses all waiting to get a scoop or two. Sabion picked Rocky Road and Brynn chose Tiger's Tail. They were in their glory. They were enjoying each other's company so much that it felt like a vacation. Brynn almost had Sebastian to thank for this trip but quickly stomped her thoughts of him out of her mind. This was her time with Sabion, and she was not going to ruin it with thoughts of Sebastian and the Decktra Corporation right now.

There was just so much beauty to see in this part of the country. Everything was so green, and the mountains were so beautiful. Brynn was in love with the countryside. If they were not running away, she would have loved to explore all the sights that they were passing. There were so many national parks, trails, and historical sights of the first railway spikes and the train that made a figure eight far down below in tunnels, to go see the Mica dam that had been built in Revelstoke and all the hot springs that they could have enjoyed. When life was back to normal, they were defiantly going to come back here for a real vacation someday. The drive from Revelstoke to Golden was outstanding. Some of the highway at times was on the very edge of a mountain and the cliffs dropped far below on the passenger side. Sometimes Brynn would feel like they were going to drive off the cliff with the twists and turns on the narrow highway, but it was all so breathtaking.

They crossed the summit and over into the Alberta Provincial Boarder. They headed through the Banff National Park and paid for a park pass, as they knew they would be stopping in Banff to spend the night. This little town was so picturesque. It was a tourist trap for sure, but it was worth it. They stopped at the 'Royal Canadian Lodge' and decided that they would splurge a bit and got a room with a Jacuzzi outside on a private balcony, a king-size bed, and a fireplace. When they entered the room, it was beautiful, and the bed was large and comfortable. They turned on the fireplace immediately. The room was sizable and yet very cozy. The feature wall was rustic, with logs and stones. The private balcony faced into the trees with a majestic mountain behind them. It was so relaxing and private. Brynn could not wait to try out the Jacuzzi with Sabion. They ordered in, and with it, Sabion ordered a nice bottle of wine. They ate a mouthwatering steak with fully loaded baked potatoes and asparagus. It was delicious. As soon as they were finished eating, Brynn turned on the smart TV and logged into her YouTube account and went to her music list. She picked out her favorite band 'Blue October' to listen to. She loved this band. The singer was so passionate, and his voice was so powerful and haunting as he sang about his real-life experiences, his addictions, and his daughter. The song 'fear' came on and it was just so appropriate for what they were going through right now.

Satisfied with her music choice, she took off all her clothes and wrapped herself in a large fluffy white bathrobe that the inn had provided in their rooms. She poured herself a glass of wine and headed out to the Jacuzzi. She made sure that Sabion was watching her as she slowly dropped the robe with a come-hither look on her face and then entered the hot water.

Sabion could not get out of his clothes fast enough. He cursed as his jeans got stuck on his feet and he stumbled around trying to get them off. He could hear Brynn's amused laughter coming from the balcony as she watched. When he was finished making a fool out of himself, he decided to slow down and grab a glass of wine as well. Only instead of donning a robe, he decided to tease her a little as he slowly walked towards her stark-naked. She smiled so beautifully at him as he entered the hot tub and she not too gently threw herself onto him as water splashed everywhere. He spun her around laughing and they then settled with her sitting on his lap with a few deep wonderful kisses. He was so happy that he could touch her now as he had always fantasized about. They fondled and kissed and just enjoyed each other but they did not make love. They soon sat beside each other and let the hot bubbling water relax them as they looked out at the gorgeous view before them, sipping on their glasses of wine.

They sat in silence for about ten minutes when Sabion cleared his throat and turned to Brynn. "Did Sebastian tell you any details about Jacklyn and Decktra to you?"

Brynn swished the water around in front of her. "Yes, he told me everything, I think."

Sabion inhaled deep and then exhaled it out. "I am thankful for that; I wasn't sure if he kept it all to himself. Would you mind telling me what he told you? Then I will tell you what I found out in Jacklyn's diary that I found in her safe and we can compare notes and fill each other in on all the details." Brynn nodded and took a sip of her wine and then exited the Jacuzzi. When they were dried, warm, and wrapped in their robes, they sat in comfortable chairs that they moved in front of the fireplace and she began her story about what had happened to her and what she had been told when she was with Sebastian.

Brynn told him everything. She told Sabion all that Sebastian had done to her and said to her and how she had tried to escape. She told him everything right down to her trying to distract him with her touch. She apologized to Sabion for that. Sabion did not blame her, as she thought at the time that he was dead, and she was doing everything in her power to keep herself safe. He also knew that she loathed having to calm him down this way. When she was finished, he then explained his side of what happened after she had been taken and what he had read in the diaries and letters. The stories of the two matched up. "I found something else in the safe as well, Brynn, and I brought it with me." Sabion stood up and went to his jacket and pulled out something wrapped in a brown paper bag. He brought it over to Brynn and he took the items out of the bag. It was a handgun; it was a nine millimeter semi-automatic handgun and a few extra clips. I only brought it with us in case something happens. Brynn reached out and glided her finger over the cold steel of the gun.

She nodded and looked up at Sabion. "I'm glad you brought that, Sabion. I feel safe with you, but this is just an added measure."

Sabion nodded, took the gun, placed it back in the bag, and put it back in his jacket pocket. "I just needed you to see it and know that it is only for safety in case you found it. I do not want you to be scared."

Brynn followed Sabion as he put the gun back in his pocket and when he turned around, she hugged him. "Thank you for coming for me, Sabion. Thank you for saving me." Sabion gathered her up in his arms and carried her to the bed and gently laid her onto it.

As he peeled back her robe, he stated, "I would do it every day for the rest of my life if it meant you would always be with me." He let his robe drop and gently lowered himself to her. They made love slowly and gently and then curled up and fell asleep facing each other as Blue October's 'I hope you're happy' played quietly in the background.

That next morning, they exited Banff National Park and continued to drive east on the TransCanada Highway. They wanted to find somewhere to stay a bit more permanently and off the beaten path. They passed through Canmore. It was so damn beautiful there. They almost wanted to stay in Canmore and find a place, but it was too close to the highway, so they decided to drive a bit more. They found a place on the map that looked like it would suit their needs and decided to turn off the highway onto Highway Twenty-two and headed south towards a small village called Bragg Creek. It was a little farther off the TransCanada Highway. Bragg Creek looked like it was secluded but still had all the facilities necessary to live nicely. Maybe they would find a little rentable cabin there. When they drove into the little village, Brynn was in love. Sure, it was a tourist spot for all the campers and off-roaders, but it was so quaint and surrounded by beautiful forest and nature.

Sabion pulled up in front of the MaxWell Realty building and Sabion told Brynn to wait. He exited the car and entered the business. There were a few people inside waiting, so Sabion approached the reception desk, leaned over, and asked the receptionist a question. When the receptionist looked up and saw Sabion leaning on the counter and was able to get over her shock at the beautiful man standing in front of her, she asked him to repeat his question. "I was wondering if you knew if there were any furnished cabins in the area that I may be able to rent on a month-to-month basis." The receptionist was just so flustered that when she reached for some papers, she spilled her coffee all over her and dropped a bunch of papers onto the floor in response. Sabion closed his eyes in frustration. He was used to this reaction, but it never got any easier, especially since they wanted to find something fast.

Sabion heard a man clear his throat behind him and then say, "I may know of something you might be interested in."

Sabion turned towards the voice and saw a man standing up from a chair he had been waiting in. "Hi, my name is Lyle. I am sorry for eavesdropping on your conversation, but I do believe she will be no help to you for a few minutes." Sabion turned to look at the poor receptionist that was cursing to herself as she cleaned up all the spilled coffee from her desk and laughed lightly.

"This is true. Hello, I am Ben Smith. Did you say you may be able to help me?"

The man stepped forward, now slightly intimated at the height and size of the man before him but continued, "I feel bad talking about this inside a realty office. Would you mind if we stepped outside?" Sabion obliged and led the man out of the office.

When they were standing in front of their car, Sabion waved at Brynn and she waved and smiled back at them both and he stated, "That's my wife."

Lyle smiled and was relieved a little that this man had a wife. It made him seem less intimidating somehow, so he continued, "I heard you were needing a cabin to rent that is furnished for a while. My niece has a cabin that is empty right now and she was telling me just yesterday that she wished she could rent it out for a bit for some extra pocket money. If you're interested, I could give you her contact information and you could tell her I sent you her way if you would like. I normally would not do this, but she and her husband have run a little down on their financial luck right now and this may help them out a little. There are so many cabins hear and the competition is a little fierce for renters. Their cabin is farther away from town though, so a lot of renters would rather be closer to town and the activities, but if you do not mind that it is a bit more secluded, it would really help her out. I am the only family she and her husband have left. I try to look out for them as much as possible wherever I can."

Sabion could not believe his luck. So far it sounded perfect. "I am very grateful to you for this information. I would really appreciate that phone number and would like to contact her as soon as possible."

Lyle took out a card from his wallet and wrote his niece's number and name on the back of it and handed it to Sabion. "Just mention my name and that I told you about the cabin so she knows how you found out about it, since she hasn't advertised about it yet."

Sabion took the card and shook Lyle's hand. "Thank you so much. My wife and I appreciate this more than you know."

Lyle tipped his head a little. "Good luck, Ben. Enjoy the rest of your day. I hope this works out for you all." Lyle then stepped back into the realty office and Sabion hopped back into the car. Lyle watched them as they backed out and smiled to himself. He only helped the young man because he figured he was a celebrity with the way he looked and dressed and wanted to keep them being here on the down low, so this was a perfect opportunity to help his niece, since they were low on money. Unfortunately, he would come to regret his decision soon; he just did not know what he was sending his niece's way.

Chapter Twenty-Two

Sabion explained to Brynn what had just transpired and they both could not believe their luck. Hopefully, they would like the cabin and it met their needs for a while. They pulled into the main shopping area of the little town and parked. Sabion turned to Brynn. "Okay, watch me work my charm as I get someone to lend me their cellphone. I just have to find the right person." It took Sabion all of thirty seconds to find his intended target and he jumped out of the car. "Stay here. I will be right back." Sabion lightly trotted over to a group of younger teen girls around the ages of sixteen and seventeen and Brynn watched him work his charm. Soon, they were handing him a phone and giggling and whispering to each other as Sabion used the cellphone. Sabion did know how to lay on the charm. Brynn felt sorry for the girls though. They would be in a tither about him for a while. When Sabion had finished with the call, he handed the phone back to the girls and thanked them by shaking all their hands gently. As he ran back to the car, Brynn watched as the girls stared after him. One girl was even waving her hand in front of her face like the beauty queens did when they won a pageant. Then they all gathered, giggling and walking towards the gas station in a group of whispering teen-girl hormones.

When Sabion entered the car again, Brynn playfully hit him in the arm. "You're so bad, babe."

Sabion just laughed, "Well, I got the use of a cellphone, did I not?"

Brynn giggled. "Those poor girls are going to be talking about you for the next week or more, you know."

Sabion just shrugged and smiled at Brynn. "I was able to get a hold of the lady Nicole that owns the cabin. She is willing to meet us out there in an hour with her husband to show us around. She gave me the directions, so we just have enough time to get some groceries and supplies, then we will go out and meet them."

Nicole and her husband, Jamie, were a young couple, not much older than they were. Brynn felt that they would become good friends, depending how long they stayed. Nicole was the same height as Brynn, and she was incredibly beautiful with long brown hair and a slim build. Jamie was surprisingly just as tall and almost as well built as Sabion due to his owning his own contracting company, so he was very fit as well. The best thing about it was she could see how in love the two were, so they never even gave much of the awkward attention that they usually received from people. They must be used to the same kind of attention, as they too were a very handsome couple.

They had all hit if off surprisingly well and Nicole and her husband were delighted to rent out their cabin to the both of them after they had been told that they were a newlywed couple that had eloped and now they wanted to just be alone with each other in the seclusion of the forest in a cabin and hide away with just each other for a while for an extended honeymoon. Nicole thought that was so romantic and they agreed on a month's stay. Sabion paid them in cash, which Nicole and Jamie very much appreciated. Sabion offered them way too much money though, but he was just making sure that they could get the place. The cabin was small but in no way uncomfortable. It was clean, cozy, and warm with a small kitchen, bathroom, and living room with a fireplace and then there were stairs that led to an open loft that contained the bedroom with a large comfortable bed. Outside the cabin had a small porch with two beautiful rocking chairs that looked out onto a small yard that was surrounded by a full forest of trees. It was quite perfect for the two of them to live in for a while. Nicole and Jamie did warn them about the bears that were quite often seen and told them to make sure any garbage that was thrown out needed to be either burned or thrown into the bear-proof garbage bin off behind the cabin.

After a bit more visiting, Nicole and Jamie left them alone to begin settling into their new space. The next few weeks were peaceful and relaxing. They had even made a trip into the city of Calgary to purchase some clothing, since they had so little between them, nothing special though, just a few outfits each for them to be out in the woods. They did not need anything fancy living out in the cabin and they would not be going out to eat or to party at all. Brynn did not mind this at all. In fact, she could stay out here forever. She loved playing the housewife and cooking and cleaning for Sabion. In the evenings, they would sit out on the patio and enjoy mother nature in its most rustic form. They even had deer every evening and morning wandering into the yard. It was just so perfect. Eventually, they would be able to go out and make friends after they were sure they had kept Sebastian and the Decktra Corporation off their backs. Sabion was very content as well. He kept himself busy chopping wood and repairing a few minor things here and there that needed to be done around the cabin to the delight of Nicole and Jamie, especially since he paid for all the materials and would not accept payment for them back.

Nicole and Jamie had come out a few times over the weeks and they were becoming great friends. Brynn found conversation with Nicole easy and they never had a lack of things to talk about. Jamie and Sabion were becoming fast friends as well. Jamie had a black belt in *taekwondo*, so they talked about this all the time and Jamie was fascinated about Sabion's fighting career and never tired of hearing Sabion tell him about his matches. Jamie even offered Sabion a job in his construction company if he ever wanted it and they decided to stay. They had even discussed possibly buying the cabin from them if they did decide to stay. There was no envy or jealousy between them, and they were just two couples enjoying each other's company and friendship. Nicole and Jamie would be coming over the next night for supper, with Nicole insisting it was their turn to bring out the food and beer. They would let the guys barbecue as they made the side dishes and just have a nice home-cooked dinner together. Such normalcy was so refreshing to Brynn. She was beginning to forget about Sebastian and why they were here in the first place.

Everything about their lives right now was perfect, except that Brynn was finding that she was not feeling so well, in the mornings especially. She hid this from Sabion though. Certain smells and foods would make her sick and she was starting to feel a little more emotional than usual. This morning, it hit her a bit harder than usual. After they had made love that morning, Brynn had to bolt to the bathroom to throw up. She was so happy right now. Why was her stomach giving her so many issues of late? She knew she still had anxiety in the back of her mind that Sebastian would find them. Maybe this was what was giving her the sour stomach and the excess of emotions. When Sabion went outside after breakfast to chop some more wood for the fireplace, Brynn sat down on the couch for a while. She was trying to read a book she had purchased in Calgary to read, but her stomach would not leave her be. She almost vaulted over the couch to get to the bathroom before she puked all over the floor. As she flushed the toilet and splashed water on her face, she suddenly had an epiphany.

Brynn exited the bathroom, and she grabbed the keys to the car and told Sabion she was just going to go into Bragg Creek to grab some toilet paper and a few supplies and she would be right back. Sabion gave her a kiss and told her to be safe. He made sure she had her hoodie up so she could conceal her face as much as possible and then off she went. Brynn was humming with anticipation. She was scared, happy, unsure, excited, and horrified all at the same time. She tried to keep herself calm until she knew for sure. Brynn pulled up to Bragg Creek Foods and got out of the car. As she headed towards the doors, she stopped. Someone was watching her; she just knew it. Casually, she looked around to see if she could spot who it was that was watching her. It was the exact same sensation she had when she and Sabion were walking on the beach by their house on Vancouver Island. She could not see anyone lurking about when she searched the parking lots and around all the vehicles. She shook her head and mumbled to herself that she was crazy and entered the store. Brynn immediately went over to the small pharmaceutical aisle. When she found what she was looking for, she just could not wait and asked to use the public washroom that needed a key to use. She waited not too patiently for three minutes after she had voided.

Two solid blue lines were before her when she looked at the pregnancy stick. She checked and double-checked the instructions on the box. She looked at the stick again. She was pregnant. She was so happy and terrified that she began to cry. *Imagine a little Sabion running around.* She would be the best mother ever and she would never lie to her child no matter what happened. She could not wait to tell Sabion. She would tell him tomorrow night after Nicole and Jamie left from their visit. She knew that Sabion would be overjoyed. This would bond them together even more than they already were. A flicker of terror splashed quickly across her brain again suddenly. *What about Sebastian? Where is he? Was it right to bring a child into their lives at such a tumultuous time,* Brynn stomped this thought out of her mind immediately. She would discuss this with Sabion tomorrow night when she told him, and they would come up with a plan together after that. She would not worry about Sebastian and their new scenario until she talked to Sabion. With her suspicions confirmed and a plan in place for when she told Sabion, she left the bathroom with a huge smile on her face. She purchased some toilet paper and a few supplies to bring back to the cabin so Sabion would not see her come back empty-handed and question her. She was so looking forward to tomorrow night and telling Sabion that they were going to have a baby. Her senses were completely overpowered with her joy that she completely missed the hooded figure leaning against a wooden pole a few feet away from the doors of the store she just exited, watching her. Brynn got back into her car, completely unaware of the man focused on her as she drove back to the cabin.

The rest of the day went smoothly but Sabion did notice a different happy energy in Brynn. When he teased her about it, she just stated that she was so happy about life now and she was just savoring their lives together. Sabion accepted this explanation and he scooped her up and vaulted up the stairs. They made love in the afternoon as the sunlight shone in from the skylight onto the center of the bed. They napped for a bit and then went outside to sit in the later afternoon sun on the porch together. Brynn found it exceedingly difficult to hide her secret. She wanted to blurt it out so many times. She began thinking that while they were sitting here so peacefully enjoying the weather right now, she might as well just tell him. Then they could celebrate tonight and talk about what they were going to do and then break the news to Nicole and Jamie tomorrow. Just as she decided to tell Sabion and leaned in to start telling him her secret, Sabion jumped up from his chair and tensely stared out, looking around into the forest. He peered into the forest and listened hard. Brynn jumped up too and stood beside Sabion with her arm linked into his. His actions scared her. He must have heard something in the trees. Just as Sabion stepped off the porch, a deer and two of her fawns darted out and ran across the lawn, startling them both. The deer ran right towards them before they quickly swerved away and off to the opposite side of the cabin. Brynn sighed with relief; this must have been what Sabion had heard but he was still on edge.

Sabion went over and grabbed an ax from the woodpile, and this had Brynn panicking a little. He told Brynn to get in the cabin and lock the door and told her not to open it for anyone but him. He then realized something and came over to whisper in Brynn's ear. "Only open the door for me if I say the word 'peacock' and get the gun out of my jacket, Brynn. Make sure you have it by you." Sabion quickly kissed Brynn and then turned her towards the cabin door. "I love you. Now lock the door." Brynn did what she was told but watched out the window as Sabion walked and disappeared into the woods in front of the cabin. Brynn was panicking as she went over to the coats hanging by the door and found the gun and unwrapped it from the paper bag. She flipped the safety off. *Thank God Sabion had shown to me how to work the gun.* He did not let her shoot it though, as they only had a few clips with bullets but he had shown and told her all the mechanics of how to work the gun, how to hold it comfortably, and how to aim it. He also showed her how to reload the gun if one clip ran out. There were fifteen rounds per clip, but he just wanted her to know how to do it and feel comfortable with the weapon.

Had Sebastian found them? Sabion must have not thought what he heard was the deer. He made sure he had a code word for her to let him back in. Sabion realized she may think that it was him coming back but it could be Sebastian. Without this code word, she could easily let in the wrong man. Brynn began to pace back and forth in front of the door. She was worried about Sabion in the forest with only an ax for a weapon. She knew about Sebastian's training and this was his element. He could easily surprise Sabion and take him down in the forest. Time ticked away and Sabion had not come back. The sun was behind the trees now and everything was getting dark in the shade of the trees. *What the hell is happening out there? Where is Sabion?*

Suddenly, there was a knock at the door and Brynn peeked out of the window with the gun in her hand. Sabion leaned forward and said 'peacock' to the door. Relief washed over Brynn and she unlocked and opened the door, throwing herself into Sabion's arms. "You had me so worried. Did you see anything?"

Sabion shook his head. "I heard something, or more so sensed something, and when the deer ran out of the wood almost straight for us before they swerved and went around the cabin, I knew that something had scared them from behind them in the trees. Something more dangerous than us. I did find out what it was though. There is a large grizzly bear roaming down around by the creek not too far away. He was a big boy for sure. Thank God we burned the garbage this morning or I think he would be on our deck right now."

Just a bear. Brynn had never been so relieved in her life. Who would have thought anyone would be relieved that there was a grizzly bear wandering around close to them? But Brynn sure was. Sabion was as well. They had both thought that Sebastian had found them. They were both still on edge a bit, so they made sure the backdoor by the fridge was secured and all the windows as well, even the one in the bathroom. Today had been a good reminder that they still were not safe in their little world that they had created. They still had to be careful. It had only been three weeks. They were not out of the woods yet.

Chapter Twenty-Three

The next day flew by without any more drama, and soon Nicole and Jamie were pulling into the driveway. They stood and visited outside for a while, since it was so nice, but soon Jamie realized that he had forgotten to pick up the beer that they had promised to bring for all of them. Sabion felt comfortable enough to leave the ladies alone for just a bit and went with Jamie into Bragg Creek to pick up some beer. When the men hopped into Jamie's truck, Nicole and Brynn ventured into the cabin to start on the side dishes. Nicole and Brynn chatted for a bit when Nicole suddenly put the knife down on the counter and turned to Brynn. "Okay, girl, spill it."

Brynn looked confused at Nicole for a minute. "Spill what?" Brynn quickly thought that Nicole had somehow found out about why Sabion and Brynn were really here. Nicole smiled and took a sip of her iced tea she had been given and leaned in towards Brynn.

"You're glowing and you can't stop smiling. You're pregnant, aren't you?" When Brynn gasped, Nicole leaned in and hugged Brynn. "I knew it the moment I saw you today. You have that look. Congratulations, does Sabion know?"

Brynn shook her head. "I only found out myself yesterday. It has only been confirmed with a pregnancy test I bought at the pharmacy. I am going to tell him tonight. I wanted to tell him immediately yesterday, but we had a scare with a big grizzly hanging around and I just forgot."

Nicole laughed. "So you finally got to see 'Big Charlie.' He has been wandering around these parts for years. He is safe, though, if you stay out of his way. You are burning the garbage like we told you to, right?"

The two women began making the side dishes again when Nicole stated, "I will help you hide your secret for tonight when they hand you a beer and you don't drink it. I will help you fill it with iced tea or something, okay?"

Brynn stopped and hugged Nicole. "I am so glad we met. You are amazing." Nicole stopped and picked up the small bin of garbage from between them, as it was getting full of cuttings from the vegetables and potato peelings.

"That's what friends are for." She headed towards the door to go to the bear safe bin. "I'll be right back, just going to put this in the garbage bin." Brynn smiled at her and kept on cutting up the potatoes for them to be cooked and mashed. She was so happy to have a friend like Nicole. She had never had a female friend before. All the girls she had ever grown up around or went to school with avoided her like the plague. It was so nice to finally have a female friend to confide in.

When Nicole came back in, Brynn looked up with a smile on her face, only for that smile to fade instantly when she saw the man standing behind Nicole with a gun pointed at her head. All the blood drained from Brynn's face. It was Sebastian. Nicole was frantic and began crying. "Where is

Jamie? Sabion, what did you do with my husband?" Nicole thought this was Sabion and Brynn could understand why.

She came around the kitchen island slowly and quietly and stated, "Nicole, I promise you, this is not Sabion."

Nicole frowned through her tears. "This is not Sabion? Are you mad? What did you do to Jamie? Where is he?"

Brynn could tell that Nicole was about to become hysterical. "Nicole, this is Sebastian, Sabion's identical twin. We were hiding here away from him, Nicole, obviously not well enough."

Nicole sobbed and Sebastian laughed. "Hello again, Brynn. I told you I would find you no matter where you tried to hide."

Nicole looked at Brynn as she realized Brynn was telling her the truth that this was not Sabion. This meant that their men were still in town or about to drive up the drive. Relief flooded through Nicole as she realized her husband was still safe. Before either of them knew what was happening, Nicole spun around. Apparently, she had taken some form of Karate training as well. The spinning kick she had just attempted almost connected with Sebastian's arm that held the gun, but he had been too quick for her. He backed up just enough and when he shot, Sebastian's bullet did not miss though as Nicole's kick had. Nicole fell to the ground in a heap on the floor.

Brynn screamed and dove towards Nicole's body, sobbing. Her poor friend had died trying to save them with a surprise attack. It had failed and now she lay on the floor dead for her efforts. Brynn knew she was dead, as half of Nicole's face was missing and blown apart where the bullet had hit her. Brynn's stomach could not take what she was seeing, and she vomited all over the floor. Sebastian just laughed. He was in killing mode now and he acted like he had enjoyed it. Brynn tried to spit on him as she kneeled beside her friend's body. Sebastian dodged the mucus and bent down to Brynn with his gun pointed at her head with a deadly look in his eyes. "This time, I am going to kill your precious Sabion just like your friend here." He grabbed Brynn and threw her onto the couch. "I have to say that you both hide from me pretty well. I am surprised. No credit card or debit withdraws. No speeding tickets or use of a cellphone or the GPS on your car. You both stayed separate and paid cash for everything. Very smart." Brynn glared at Sebastian as he paced back and forth in front of the couch, waving the gun around like it was a toy.

Brynn had to ask, "Then how did you find us, Sebastian?"

Sebastian stopped pacing and kneeled in front of Brynn, making sure the gun was still pointed at her. "You see, the amazing good looks that the three of us possess is extremely hard for people to ignore. It makes everyone giddy and they get all hot and bothered when we are around them or they see us. They seem to think they are in the presence of a celebrity, so they just can't help taking pictures and posting them all over Instagram, Tic Toc, Facebook and all the other social media sights that are out there." Sebastian laughed again. "At first, I was having a hard time finding you after I dislocated my thumb and got out of the cuffs. I also had another key in my shirt pocket for the ankle cuffs that Sabion conveniently did not check for. Thank you very much for that by the way for leaving me to rot. I will have to punish you for that one when we get back to Decktra and train you to be a good girl." Sebastian tried to lean forward and kiss Brynn. Just then, she attempted to slap him, only for him to slap her hard first. She saw spots flash before her eyes for a moment. "I was far too soft with you the first time around. Do not think I will be this time." Sebastian stood up again and continued his story as he pulled his cellphone out and began flipping through it.

He laughed again as he turned the phone for her to see the screen. "This one is a good one of you and Sabion in a restaurant in Vancouver with the question posted on Instagram from 'Nikki': *'Does anyone know who these two beautiful people are and if they are famous or not?'*" Sebastian flipped to another photo and it was of Brynn. "I do love this one of you all bright-eyed and bushytailed posted by Derek from Kamloops, stating: *'Just saw the most beautiful woman in the world. She is now my new poster girl for my wall.'*" Sebastian showed her one more. "Love this one. It is my favorite, as it is a complement to me as well in a roundabout way." It was a photo of Sebastian eating ice cream in Sicamous. "This one has the post, *'Step aside, Jason Momoa. There's a new stud in town.'* I do love that one. You see, Brynn, I couldn't find you with all the traditional ways, with all the fancy computer tracking of cellphones and security cameras, so I figured about a few days ago to check all the social sites, and bam! There you both were in all the places that you stopped. It was like reading a map, Brynn. All this social media bullshit led me right to you. I did lose you after you left Banff though, until some sweet young sixteen-year-old from Bragg Creek of all places posted this one of Sabion using her friend's cellphone. Silly chit did not post it till the other day though, or I would have been here much sooner.

"I did end up finding some security footage from a little relator company of Sabion in front of the building, shaking the hand of dear Lyle as he handed Sabion a card. Poor Lyle! He did not die quietly before I extracted the information I needed from him to get the location of this cabin." Brynn lowered her head, saddened by the news. *Another person dead because of this maniac.*

Brynn cringed; they had tried to be so careful. Not once had she ever thought about their pictures being taken from people during their drive to get away would ever end up splashed all over social media for Sebastian to track them with. *Oh God!* She was going to be sick again, but just then, she could hear a truck coming up the drive and she gasped. Sebastian heard it as well. Brynn tried to jump off the couch over the back and run out the front door to warn the men, but Sebastian was much too fast for her. He grabbed her and punched her in the face hard. She was temporarily dazed and almost passed out. Sebastian stood behind the couch in front of the door and, without hesitation, shot the first person that entered the doorway. It had been Jamie and his body crashed right on top of his wife's body and the beer he had been carrying flew out of his hand and smashed everywhere.

Sabion did not hesitate. When he heard the shot as he came up the porch behind Jamie. As soon as he heard the shot and saw Jamie fall, his fighting instinct kicked in immediately and he dove into the front door, knocking Sebastian down as he flew over the two bodies on the floor. Sebastian had been a little pissed off that it had not been

Sabion and for a split-second took his eyes off the door to see that it was Jamie lying on the body of the woman instead of Sabion. This gave just enough time for Sabion to attack without getting shot. Sebastian's gun flew out of his hand and landed near the bathroom. It sounded like two bears were trying to tear each other apart.

As they fought, they knocked over the couch that Brynn was lying dazed on and she was spilled onto the throw carpet, narrowly missing smashing her head on the heavy coffee table. Brynn struggled to get out from under the couch. She had to find a way to save them both. Her lying on the floor in a daze would not help either of them now. She pulled herself together and shook off the fog from the punch that Sebastian had dealt her with. She was so angry and scared. She had to avoid the two men as they threw each other around the room. Her eyes fell on the gun lying on the floor forgotten by the bathroom and she went straight for it. When she had the gun, she pointed it at the two of them with trembling hands. She could not figure out who was who. She could not shoot because she did not know which one was which, as they conveniently were both wearing a white t-shirt and jeans.

Brynn was frantic. They would kill each other if she did not figure something out immediately. How could she figure out which one was Sebastian so she could shoot him? She had to figure this out extremely fast, as either Sabion or Sebastian was now getting the upper hand and was choking the life out of the other one. *Think. Think.* In her fear, her brain suddenly became crystal-clear. She began to see images of her unborn child in her head and all the wonderful days and nights of passionate lovemaking that Sabion and she had enjoyed. She bombarded her brain with all the fantastic kisses and how hard she had climaxed with Sabion every time they had made love. She bombarded her brain with how much she loved his hands touching her and caressing her. She flooded her mind with how she had found out that she was pregnant, and she was carrying Sabion's unborn child in her womb.

It worked. Sebastian whirled off Sabion's nearly unconscious body and growled as he turned towards Brynn. There was an anguished pain in Sebastian's eyes as he slowly stalked towards her as she held the gun on him. "That was supposed to be my child you carry. You were made for me, Brynn. How could you do this to me?" He lunged at her, but she pulled the trigger and the bullet entered Sebastian's shoulder. He did not go down though. Sebastian looked at the bullet hole in his shirt and then looked at Brynn, a little shocked. "I did not think you had that in you, good girl." He lunged again and this time, Brynn aimed at his head.

Sebastian dropped with a sickening thud onto the ground beside Jamie and Nicole's bodies. The large hole on his forehead confirmed to Brynn he was indeed dead. She dropped the gun and quickly went over to Sabion who was trying to catch his breath and was struggling to get up. Brynn did not care as she grabbed him and held on for dear life in a bone-crushing hug. She only let go when she heard Sabion gasp in pain. When she pulled away to look at him, he was covered in blood and cuts from all over his face.

"Man, did that bastard know how to hit?" Sabion coughed out and then he grabbed his ribs. "I think he broke a few of my ribs as well." Sabion looked over at Sebastian lying dead on the floor and then looked at Brynn thoughtfully. "How the hell did you manage to get him off me? If you had not, I would not be talking to you right now. He was an animal. Everything I threw at him, he was able to break out of and give one back. He had me, Brynn. He was about to kill me."

"Remember in the hotel room in Banff, I told you everything that Sebastian had told me and one of those things was that he could read minds. I just bombarded my head with thoughts of you and us together and focused them towards Sebastian and just kept doing it over and over in my head but I was focused so hard on him, I think, that he could not keep me out of his head."

Sabion frowned and just shook his head. "So, it was true then. He could read minds. When you told me that, I just assumed he had been lying to you and just got lucky with a few things to convince you. Jesus! That's crazy, and you…you were amazing, Brynn. That was genius to think of that." Sabion groaned again as he tried to put his arm around Brynn. "God, I hurt all over." Brynn helped Sabion stand up and they hugged each other. Sabion pulled away and held Brynn's face with both his hands and leaned his forehead against hers. "Now it is my turn to thank you for saving for my life. Thank you, my love." They stood that way for a few minutes until Sabion sighed and pulled away, wincing. "We must leave here, Brynn. Decktra may be right behind Sebastian. He may not have come alone."

Chapter Twenty-Four

Brynn sighed and pulled away as she nodded. She looked towards Jamie and Nicole's bodies and let a few tears fall. They were dead because of the crazy maniac that was lying dead beside them. They were also dead because Brynn and Sabion had let the couple get close to them. Brynn loved the friendship that she had started with Nicole. They should have made them stay away till they knew Sebastian was out of the picture. It never occurred to her that they were putting anyone in danger. Brynn sighed again. Decktra could be here any moment. What were they going to do? Suddenly, she had an idea. Her idea pained her but Nicole and Jamie were already dead. Her plan may even benefit both her and Sabion to get Decktra to think that it was both herself and Sabion that were dead. She just had to put her plan into quick action.

Sabion was slumped against the couch wincing in pain still so Brynn ran upstairs and packed a few of their clothes and the cash and quickly took them out to the car. She picked up and put Sebastian's gun back in his cold dead hand. After Brynn arranged Sebastian and the gun she went out to the small garden shed and grabbed a full gas canister and placed it by the front door that she left open. Sabion watch her for a bit as he regained some of his strength but then pulled himself away from the couch and stopped Brynn. "Hun, what are you doing?" Brynn was a little breathless but explained herself and her idea. Sabion again grabbed her face and gently kissed her. His Brynn was brilliant. This plan just might work. They just may be free from Decktra's continued search for them as well if everything worked out.

Sabion helped Brynn put the plan into action and then when they were done, they both staged their car. They made sure they left evidence in the car of their wallets that had their photo IDs in them so it would prove that this was their car and that they were the bodies that were dead in the cabin. They took all identification off Nicole's and Jamie's bodies and kept their ID's for themselves. This hurt them both mentally, but they had to do it for this to work. Sabion started Jamie's truck and moved it away from the cabin in order to keep away from the blast. When Brynn was sure the scene was set and everything was covered, she took out Sabion's gun he had taken from Jacklyn's safe, she leaned out the open window of the truck and shot a bullet directed at the gas can that she had left by the open door. When the gas canister blew up they ducked from the blast wave. Brynn waited a moment for the flames to really catch, went up to the cabin as close as she could, and tossed the gun back in towards the bodies through the open door of the cabin. Brynn turned and hoisted herself up into the truck and for a moment, they allowed themselves a few seconds to watch the cabin being consumed by the hot, hungry flames before they pulled the truck out of the driveway and drove away, heading east.

Several hours later, back at the cabin, a tall, slim, gray-haired agent in an expensive suit and black coat exited a black unmarked SUV after they pulled up and stopped in front of a burned out smoking, husk of what remained of the little cabin. He flashed a badge quickly to the police and firemen that were surrounding the area. He was very official looking so no one on the scene even attempted to stop and question him of who and why he was there. The cops figured this man was a probing agent here to help with the investigation. They were all inexperienced with this kind of homicide. The official looking gray-haired agent approached one of the younger police officers inquiring who was in charge. The young officer pointed him in the direction of the police chief. The grey-haired agent then flashed his badge again to the chief of police when he approached him. He explained that he was from the Canadian Security Intelligence Service Agency and he was sent here to inquire on the details He explained that someone of national security may have been involved and was allegedly one of the bodies in the cabin. This certain person also may have be involved with this crime. The grey-haired agent listened as the chief went over a few details with him. The police chief was impressed. He was just an officer of a small town that had never had a triple homicide before and was out of his element with this one, so he explained what they had found hoping to get some answers or at least some assistance.

"We found three bodies inside the cabin. They have all been shot. Two males and one female. The coroner says that all three of the victims were in their early-to-mid-twenties. We also found two badly charred handguns as well. We managed to get a serial number off one of the guns. The agent asked if he could see the serial number and the police chief looked it up and handed it to the agent. The agent quickly entered it into his iPad he carried and found that the serial number matched the owner as one Jacklyn O'Connell's handgun. The agent knew that name very well. When the agent was done he asked the chief to continue. We searched the car left here on the scene and found two of the victims' IDs in it. One of the male victims in the fire was named Sabion O'Connell and the female victim was one Brynn O'Connell. We have not found any identification for the other male victim in the cabin though. We are thinking it may have been a murder, suicide, or possibly an angry lover catching his or her husband or wife in the act. The bodies are badly burned though, but the coroner declares that they all died from their gunshot wounds and we surmise that one of the bullets must have ricochet and hit a full gas can that was in the cabin near the door. This is why the cabin burned up as fast and bad as it did."

The grey-haired agent asked if he could take a quick look around the cabin and the police chief nodded. "Just be careful; the steps are no longer too sturdy, and the floor is pretty burned up and unstable." The agent entered the burned cabin and looked around a bit and then noted the three bodies. He bent down to get a closer look and noticed that the two male bodies were the exact same height and size, and the female was around the same height and size as Brynn would have been as well. He sighed. 'What a loss! Sebastian had gotten into it over his head this time and now they are all dead.' They had given Sebastian one more chance at finding Brynn and Sabion when he had called them and explained to them what had transpired. Sabion had promised he would bring the girl back. Now they were all gone. Well, at least they still had the other children at the facility, but what a shame it was to have lost such a great soldier and the adult sup female! Well, that was tragic as well.

The grey-haired agent turned and exited the burned-out cabin. He thanked the police chief and headed back to the SUV and got into the back seat. The SUV drove off quickly. The grey-haired agent picked up his cellphone and dialed the Decktra Corporation. When the phone was answered, he immediately was questioned, "Well, was it them?"

The grey-haired agent stated what he had found at the scene to the voice on the other end of the phone. "Yes! Sebastian, Brynn, and Sabion, all in the cabin, shot to death and burned." The man on the other end cursed loudly.

"Get back to the facility. There is nothing that we can do now. Let us move on and focus on the ones we still have and forget that this failure ever happened."

The grey-haired agent replied, "Yes sir," and then he hung up the phone.

Epilog

"Sable and Eden, you little rascals, you get back here." The two-year-old identical twin girls giggled and tried to run away from Sabion as he chased after them. He scooped them both up into his strong arms as they squealed in delight. "Daddy's got you now. What do you think your mother would say if she found out you were trying to sneak some of her freshly baked cookies without asking? I know she told you scampers' hands off!" Brynn walked into the kitchen and watched the scene before her with a smile on her face. Nothing made her happier than to see her beautiful family all together.

When the girls saw their mother, they squirmed to get down and ran towards her. "Mommy, cookie pweease," the twins said in unison as they waddled towards her.

She broke down and grabbed them one each from the counter and started to hand them over, but before she did, she said, "Give me a kiss first and then you can have a cookie." They both rushed to kiss their mom, and after their mission was complete, they were rewarded with a big chocolate chip cookie and rushed away to eat their prize.

Sabion walked over to his wife and gave her a kiss as they watched their two precious toddlers happily munching their cookies on the kitchen floor. "Well, I have to get back to work, sweetheart. The men get a little lazy when I am not on the site. Thank you so much for lunch. I will see you tonight. I love you." Sabion left the kitchen after he gave his munchkins a kiss. Brynn watched as Sabion entered his work truck with the large logo on the side of the door that read, *'Jamie Trevense Problem Solvers Construction,'* and sighed. Sure, they were living with the stolen identities of their friends from the tragedy in Bragg Creek. Sabion was now known as Jamie Trevense and she was his wife, Nicole Trevense. They had settled on a small acreage twenty minutes away from the city of Anchorage Alaska. Sabion was running a small construction company that was doing very well, and Brynn was a stay-at-home mom. Their lives were simple and easy, exactly the way they both wanted it. There was no drama, and it was peaceful. This was all Brynn had ever dreamed for in her life. She had so much love with Sabion, a beautiful quaint log home, and most importantly, her beautiful daughters that looked exactly like their daddy. When her children were old enough, Brynn and Sabion would sit them down and tell them everything and where they truly came from. Brynn would never hide such a secret from her children. They had a right to know when they were old enough. Brynn smiled as she watched her two chubby little twins stuffing chocolate chip cookies into each other's mouths. Life could not be more normal, and Brynn could not be any happier than she was at this very moment.

As a smiling Brynn looked away from her chubby twins with melted chocolate all over their mouths and hands and back out to the driveway to watch the tail end of Sabion's truck drive away, the phone rang. She sighed and got up to answer the phone. "Problem Solvers Construction, Nicole speaking." A deep, older, male voice on the other end of the line spoke slowly, "Hello. It is so good to finally hear your voice, Brynn." All the breath left Brynn's chest and her voice caught in her throat. All the feeling left her body and the phone slipped from her grasp. The phone shattered in several pieces as it hit the floor. The twins startled at the loud noise and began to cry. All Brynn could do was stare at her two little angels and an instant fear for their lives bubbled to the surface and her happiness shattered into a million pieces. It was Decktra. They had found them once again.

The End